Broken Code

Book 3 of the Benton Security Services series
by Christine Shuck

Jack Benton Can Kiss My...

- Lila -

The bell over the front door jangled in time with the ice-cold blast of wind and Angela, wrapped head to toe, snow dusting her knit cap.

Lila shivered and pulled her cardigan closer. The wind raced along the street, and at the height of winter, it was especially frigid. Angela was late, as usual. Even in winter, the girl couldn't make it to work on time.

"Oh my God, the weather is really taking a turn for the worse." Angela said, shivering and stomping her feet to avoid tracking it across the front of the store.

Margery, who had been waiting impatiently for Angela to arrive, levered herself out of a nearby chair. "You're late. Again."

Angela peered at her through a static-filled billow of hair that stuck out and waved wildly now that she released it from the knit cap. "Um... sorry?" She replied. Her tone sounded put-upon, more than truly sorry, and Lila hid a smirk as Margery rolled her eyes in Lila's direction.

"Right, well, I'm off to lunch and my appointment. See you tomorrow... oh wait, are you leaving tonight?" She waggled her eyebrows. "With Hubba Hubba hot guy?"

Lila grinned. "He's flying in tonight. We'll leave the day after tomorrow. Are you sure you'll be okay to open tomorrow? If not, I can swing by and do it."

Margery waved her fingers dismissively at Lila. "Don't you dare. Take the time, relax, for once! This baby has another month to go before he's due to make an appearance. I can use all the hours you'll give me until then." She ran a hand along her rounded belly and sighed. "I can open tomorrow and through the rest of the week. I just hope that Angela here will be on time every day."

"Oh, absolutely. Not a problem." Angela answered, unwinding a scarf that had to be six feet long. Her blond hair was dancing in a halo around her head and Lila could see the snaps of electricity arc. It was dry, far drier than she had thought it would be this close to the ocean.

Margery met Lila's eyes and shook her head. It was quite clear she had no faith in the younger woman's ability to make it to her shift on time. Which was no surprise, really, since if Angela showed up at the appointed time, it would be the first time. Lila wasn't sure what she was going to do when Margery had her baby next month. She'd been advertising for weeks and no one seemed interested. She could handle running the store on her own, with Angela's infrequent and unreliable appearances, but with the first book done and published, she was eager to start on the second book in the series. It was easier with another body in the store. Even during winter, which was the slowest season, she barely had enough time to handle the unboxing of deliveries, running the cash register, and all the other sundry details that it took to keep the store running. As it was, even now she handled the financial aspects at home, a time she preferred to be writing or spending time with Shane when he was in between assignments.

The last year had been hard. Maintaining a relationship with Shane absent more than he was there, had certainly pushed her to her limits. Each time he went away, she found it harder to say goodbye.

"Okay, out I go!" Margery said, and slid her parka hood over her head, clutching the front ends of it tight over her middle. Her belly prevented her from zipping it up. She waddled out the door, and the bell overhead gave a frenzied jingle while another gust of frigid air and flying snow blasted in. Lila watched as she half ran to her car and slid in. Seconds later, the car disappeared down the street into a wall of white.

"Okay, I'm just about finished up with the book order I need to make and then I need to get to Hanniford's for a few essentials." Lila told Angela, who had unwrapped her multiple layers and secured them in the back office.

"Will you be okay to close up today?" She asked the girl and Angela nodded. "You're sure?"

"Absolutely. Don't worry, Boss. I got you covered."

"Okay. Maeve should be in soon. She asked for me to hold *Midnight at the Blackbird Cafe* for her. It's in its usual place."

Angela saluted and settled herself on the stool behind the cash register.

Lila couldn't help it; she was really looking forward to Shane's visit. He'd been gone five weeks this time, with a grueling assignment. He had said little about it, just that he was really looking forward to the two weeks off. She smiled at the thought of the surprise she had waiting for him. A trip to Sugarloaf, a full week in an Airbnb, in a *caboose* no less! She had been seconds away from sharing the link and showing him, ever since he told her about train-watching as a kid. She just knew he would love it. But she'd stopped. It was going to be a surprise. She couldn't wait to see his face when they arrived.

There will be skiing, sure, but also all the time in the world to curl up in the caboose, just the two of us.

The bell jingled and the icy blast of wind and snow hit. The thought of just how they would keep each other warm helped Lila brave the elements. She pulled her coat tighter around her as she skittered and slid through the snow to reach her car. She really hoped Angela wouldn't let her down or make it too difficult on Margery.

Although what I am going to do for full-time help once Margery's baby comes, I do not know. I really doubt that Angela will ever be dependable.

Shane had turned down her offer to pick him up at the airport. "I can catch an Uber. It's on Benton Security Services dime, anyway. No need to drive in the snow. Besides, I need to run an errand first."

The sun was already beginning to fade from the sky by the time she ran a couple of errands and pulled into the driveway. These days, the sun was gone by 4:30 and didn't reappear until seven in the morning. She hated winter for that very reason. Practically her entire day spent inside, and by the time it was over, it was already dark. Today, however, she welcomed the sunset and darkness. It meant that Shane would be here soon.

At a quarter to six, headlights illuminated the drive, and she rushed to the door to find Shane grinning at her, the thick snow already settling in a moist layer across his broad shoulders. His backpack was slung over one shoulder, his hands filled with grocery bags. She grinned as she spied a bouquet tucked under his arm.

He leaned in and captured her lips in a kiss.

"Are those for me?" She asked, taking the bags from him as he wrestled with his boots.

"Nah, I figured I'd give them to your roommate."

"Well, lucky me, I don't have a roommate." She also didn't have a vase yet, she kept forgetting to order one. The bouquet was exquisite, the roses were a lovely shade of lavender mixed with a spray of white baby's breath.

I really, really need to buy a vase.

Shane laughed as Lila reached for the tall metal cup that sat under her chrome Hamilton Beach milkshake mixer. It was that or a Contigo, and she only had the one.

"What? It works!" She busied herself with unwrapping the bouquet and adjusting the positioning of the flowers after she filled it up with water.

"I thought you were going to buy a vase."

"I keep meaning to, really I do."

Meanwhile, the stainless-steel milkshake cup was the perfect height. Lila finished futzing with the flowers and set it in the middle of the small dining room table. They looked good there. And it was a far better use for the milkshake cup. She still remembered the first time she had used it. She had tried to make a boozy shake with the mixer, gotten the measurements all wrong, and given herself the hangover of a lifetime on a vodka root beer float. At that point, the mixer, as cute as it looked there on the countertop, was relegated to household decor status. And because Shane always brought her flowers, and she had nothing else to put them in, even when he visited, the silly thing remained unused.

Shane's arms enveloped her from behind as he nuzzled her neck. His nose was ice cold, thanks to the wintry mix outside her warm, cozy house. She squirmed in his embrace.

"Two weeks. Alone. You and me."

She turned around, slipped her arms around his waist and kissed him deep, hungry. He responded in kind, his hands moving gently at first, then matching her with intensity. They moved from her hips to her back and then reached down, pulling her up, both hands firmly cupping her butt, her feet off the ground, her legs wrapping around his waist as his tongue melded with hers.

They had been apart more than they were together, but even after six months, the attraction hadn't slackened. She still felt a surge of desire every time he looked in her direction.

Shane walked forwards, holding her, his mouth devouring hers, until they crashed into the kitchen island. The bags full of groceries crinkled and shifted. He had done a decent amount of shopping. She could see that, although right now, her mind was only on one thing, and it wasn't food. She slipped a hand inside of his jeans, her fingers sliding along his flesh. His breathing changed, accelerated, and he sat her on the counter, swearing as something round and green went tumbling to the floor.

"I was going to fix dinner first." He reached for the fallen produce. Something that resembled a fat green onion teetered on the counter's edge, and he caught it before it fell.

Lila grabbed his shirtsleeve. "I love your cooking almost as much as I love other more energetic pursuits, but your priorities are all messed up, Shane Ellis." She pulled him back towards her. "Forget the lettuce."

"It's cabbage, actually..." He stopped talking as she pulled his mouth to hers and reached down to make sure the vegetable escape hadn't affected something far more vital.

Nope, his priorities are still right where they need to be.

He sucked in a breath as she undid the top button of his jeans and eased the zipper down. He set down the fat onion and returned to running his hands along her body. Roaming, exploring, possessing her in ways no man had ever done. Sex, hell, the lead-up to sex, was more thrilling than anyone she had ever been with. He reached up her skirt, his fingers questing. She shuddered as his fingers slid past the edge of her underwear and caressed her clit. A surge of dampness and she moaned against his mouth, pushing closer and closer until she risked slipping off of the edge of the counter. His erection tented his briefs, and he slipped his dick out of his bindings with one hand, the other continuing to caress her slick folds.

Lila wanted him inside her. Wanted to feel every bit of him fill her. She wrapped a hand around his silken shaft, teasing and tantalizing, listening to his breathing speed up, matching hers. The long weeks away from him had served only to build the sexual tension, and add fire to this moment here between them. Shane broke contact with her mouth and moved his lips to her neck, moving up to her earlobe where his teeth nipped her gently.

"Woman, you drive me insane. I was going to seduce you over a delectable dinner, dessert, and right now all I want to do is fuck you, right here, right now." He growled into her ear and nipped it again, harder this time.

Lila shivered, a wanton shiver she felt from the top of her head down to her toes.

She stroked him harder, slipped off the edge of the countertop, knowing he would catch her, hold her.

"You know me. I like to work up an appetite first."

A groan of frustration, lust, or perhaps both, was the only sound he made before he pushed his way inside her. A parade of groceries crashed to the floor, ignored by them both, as he thrust hard, and fast, into her. She could feel the tip of him slam into her cervix, his fingers from one hand dancing along her clit, sending waves of exquisite pleasure cresting through her as he pushed her back against the countertop.

Lila shoved a package away from the small of her back, moaned and wrapped her legs around his ass as he fucked her hard and fast. God, she had missed this! Shane ticked all the boxes for her, and the sex was simply out of this world.

Their two bodies moved as one now, both questing for the release, when the stars and planets aligned. She heard something else clatter to the floor, ignored it. She was so close. From the change in his breaths, so was he.

"Come in me now." Lila breathed, gasping in pleasure as she felt the orgasm flow through her, a wave cresting at its apex, and Shane cried out a millisecond later, groaning as he joined her. His body breaking and collapsing onto her as he rode the same wave with her.

Seconds, a moment passed. His hair tickled her bare chest. Lila sighed with pleasure. She barely remembered ripping her t-shirt off, or Shane's quick release of her bra. The oxytocin and dopamine rush were still circulating through her. She could feel it all the way through to the tips of her toes.

Shane groaned, nestled his face in her stomach, mumbled. "I love fucking you. I want to fuck you all night long, woman."

Lila smiled. "I'm good with that. As long as dinner is involved."

"I had a magnificent dinner planned. Veal scallopini with lemon and capers, potato and leek soup, and a crème brûlée for dessert."

On cue, her stomach rumbled, and he raised his head, quirked an eyebrow, and chuckled.

"I told you I wanted to work up an appetite. Well, now that I have..."

Shane's chuckle turned into a roar of laughter. He stood up, pulled his jeans back up, and straightened his clothes. Then he pulled her up against him, kissed her deeply, and set her back on the floor.

Lila reached for her t-shirt and bra, which was hanging off the corner of the butcher block next to the fat green onions. Before she could put them on, Shane pulled her into another hungry, lingering kiss.

"I cannot get enough of you, Lila. When I'm on assignment, all I can do is think about when I can see you again."

She smiled. "I feel the same way."

The corner of his mouth quirked up. "Are you sure you aren't just keeping me around for my cooking?"

Lila fastened her bra and slid her shirt back on. "Mm, a distinct possibility." She reached for the weird vegetable that was now on the floor. "This is the fattest green onion I have ever seen."

Shane snorted, "That's a leek, you uneducated heathen."

Their banter continued as he pulled out pans and pots and began working on dinner. An hour later, Lila groaned as she slipped the last spoonful of crème brûlée into her mouth. "This is almost better than sex." She caught Shane's look of dismay. "*Almost*, I said almost!"

Shane looked nonplussed, then arched an eyebrow, stood up from the table, and walked the two steps over to her. "I'll show you something far better than food, woman. It's nine inches long..."

"Eight." Lila interrupted.

"Nine. You caught me on an off day." He pulled her up to him and she could feel him growing hard. "As I was saying, I'm going to show you all nine inches of something better than food. And I'm going to do it slowly. You will beg me to finish you off." He growled in her ear.

Lila's breath caught in her throat as his mouth descended onto hers. She could taste the caramel and cream from the crème brûlée, and a hint of the lemony remnants of the veal. And, as if she hadn't already experienced one of the more memorable orgasms of her life, her body hummed with anticipation.

She reached for his hand and pulled him after her to the upstairs bedroom.

The next morning was just as satisfying. After a quickie, Lila slid from the bed, sated, and slipped into the shower. When she returned, Shane was gone from it. From the sound of it, he was busy in the kitchen again. A tantalizing aroma meandered its way up the stairs. Lila sniffed the air.

Mm. Bacon and maple syrup. I wonder if Shane knows how to make pecan pie?

She floated down the stairs, her long hair wrapped in a towel, and a thick, warm robe and slippers were the only clothing she needed.

He grinned as she entered the kitchen. "Hey Sexy, did you work up an appetite?"

"Always. It smells amazing, as usual."

"French toast with cinnamon and maple syrup. The bacon is cooking in the fridge." He swirled the pan. "The snowfall really added up. I figure the storm laid down four inches, maybe more, by the looks of it. And we have a two-hour drive in the best of conditions ahead of us. What time is check-in?"

Lila grinned. She couldn't wait to see his face when they arrived at the caboose Airbnb. "Three p.m. but she said we could come as early as two if we needed to."

"Perfect. We can eat breakfast in bed, make love until noon, shower, and leave."

Lila giggled. "Well, it sounds like the perfect start to our week-long skiing vacation!"

She leaned in to kiss him, but at that moment, his cell phone rang with a thumping melody. There was only one person it could be. Lila's heart sank as the tune yodeled, "Big, big, big boss."

Shane pulled away, dug the phone out of his jeans pocket and answered it. "Ellis here."

Lila couldn't hear what Jack Benton was saying. She didn't need to. The look on Shane's face was clear.

Are you kidding *me?*

She mouthed at Shane to tell his boss to find someone else.

"Yeah, I understand. Right. No, I'll be there. Yeah. Okay." He hung up the phone and stared at the French toast in the pan, avoiding meeting Lila's incredulous gaze.

"He did not tell you to come in. Tell me he didn't."

"Look, I have to go. It's a domestic battery situation. Wife of the chief of police. WitSec won't get involved and…"

"Tell him to find someone else!"

"There isn't anyone else. Everyone else is on assignment. He says it will only be for a week, and…"

"A week?!" Lila spat, furious and on the verge of tears. Her plans, all the plans she had made. The Airbnb she had rented. The dinner reservations at a nearby Italian restaurant, the ski package. They wouldn't be able to reschedule. There would be no one to watch the store in another few weeks other than Angela, and she was completely unreliable.

The happy, satisfied feeling she had gone to bed with, woken up with, with Shane by her side, it dissolved as if it hadn't ever really existed.

An hour later, Shane's phone dinged. He checked it. "The Uber is almost here."

Lila said nothing. She was too angry and heartbroken.

Damned if I'm going to make this easy on him, either. He just bends over for Benton. Lets him do whatever he wants, ask whatever he wants.

Shane had tried to explain. But Lila didn't want to hear it. She didn't care that there was no one else to do the job. Benton had promised Shane two weeks off. She didn't care about the reasons Shane felt he owed Jack Benton. After five years of dedicated service, he had damned well paid that debt, no matter the circumstances.

"Maybe you can get a refund on the Airbnb you rented?" His expression looked hopeful. Which merely infuriated her more.

Fuck the refund. Tell Jack to go suck an egg!

Lila settled for making a noncommittal, "Sure, whatever."

Shane shouldered his backpack. The Uber pulled up at the curb and he stared at it for a moment, then back at Lila.

"I really am sorry, Lila. If I had a choice, I'd tell him to find someone else, but I owe Jack. He needs me."

Lila closed her eyes and willed away the gathering tears.

Jack doesn't need you. I need you.

"Right." She opened them, and Shane's eyes bored into hers. Begging forgiveness and understanding. But she had neither to offer him.

He kissed her as the Uber honked impatiently. "I have to go now."

"Yeah, I know."

He stepped down onto the stoop and turned around at her again. "I'll make this up to you."

"Right." The effort to say anything felt as if she were chewing on sharp glass.

"Okay. I'll call you tonight."

She nodded, and he walked away. As he opened the door to the Uber, Lila couldn't take it anymore. She cupped her hands and called out, "Shane?"

Shane stopped and turned.

"The next time you talk to Jack Benton? You tell him I said to kiss... my... ass." She felt a small measure of satisfaction in watching Shane's eyebrows shoot up and his mouth fall open before she stomped back inside and slammed the door closed behind her.

She pressed her back against the door and let loose a string of profanity that would have shocked the townspeople, her employees, and likely even Shane. And with it came angry, hot tears of frustration.

It had taken her nearly three days to form the words and just say it. To tell him it was over. Whatever "it" was.

Long-distance relationships don't work. He picked his work over a relationship with me.

She had gathered her courage, called him, told him she couldn't do it anymore. He had said little. But really, what was there to say, anyway? It would not work. Not like this.

She missed Kaylee. She hadn't been able to talk to her friend for nearly two years. Kaylee would have told her to drop sexy pecan pie Shane Ellis like a rock. She would have taken her for sushi at Nara's and they would have gotten tipsy and gone dancing, just the two of them. But she was here, in Maine, living under an assumed name, and prohibited from contacting anyone. Angela was too young and unreliable to talk to. And Margery centered entirely on bringing a new human into the world and focusing on being a stay-at-home mom.

Lila had never felt more alone than she did now. Even when her mom had died, she could return to college, and Kaylee had been there. To listen, to hold her when she cried, and make her laugh when the time was right. This time, she was alone in her misery. She took the week off of work, if only because she didn't want to explain it to Margery or Angela. Later she could explain, when time had spooled out and the hurt and anger had diminished.

The groceries Shane had filled her fridge with eventually spoiled. Every day since he'd left, she would stand in the kitchen, refrigerator door open, and glare at the various packages. Angry, frustrated, and ultimately too depressed to even try to do anything with it all. After a week, she went to Hanniford's and purchased her regular heat and eat meals. They filled the freezer, and she stopped opening the fridge section except to grab milk for her cereal. By the third week, the smell was unbearable. She waited until the night before trash pickup and dumped the reeking mess into the Pay-As-You-Throw blue trash bags and taken to the curb while trying desperately not to breathe the stench in.

"Damn you, Shane Ellis. Kowtowing to your boss. Who cares if Jack Benton is a billionaire used to getting his way and to hell with anyone else's feelings?" She muttered angrily as she trudged back along the icy driveway. "Jack Benton can kiss my ass!"

Not Optimal

- Shane -

Her mouth moved under his, her tongue flicking, twining with his. Her body and hair, silky smooth, a tantalizing hint of vanilla and musk, moved against his. God, he wanted her, always her, and the thoughts of any other woman were half-measures, poor substitutions.

He moved from her mouth to her neck, just at the ear, and Lila writhed under him, her fingernails digging into his back. Her body was begging for more. The soft pants and moans had him hard. He slid down her body, his feet catching on the sheets. He tried to kick them away, once, twice.

And then his dream splintered into fragments. Shane woke instantly, alert in the dark night, and alone in the bed. Something had woken him, but what?

As with all of his assignments, Shane quickly came to identify every creak and groan of a safe house. Noises that meant nothing to the newest occupants. A certain squeak of floorboard, the smallest click of a doorknob turning in place. A change in air pressure that showed someone had opened an exterior door. Or someone in the hall outside of his bedroom.

He moved without sound. Slipping from his bed, clad in his boxers, his 9mm Ruger held in his right hand, easing the safety off. Shane knew better than most that one's fate can be measured in milliseconds. Whoever was entering his room wouldn't know the layout and likely wasn't expecting him to be awake. This was to his advantage. The heavy rain outside held no lightning, nothing to add anything but darkness to the already gloomy sky outside.

The doorknob gave itself away with a small, nearly imperceptible click. Whoever was outside in the hall was coming in. In the brief half-second between the doorknob turning, and the door quietly opening, he caught the scent, or rather the reek, of the girl's perfume, which preceded her entry.

The light in the hall illuminated just enough of the Ruger for Heather Bonatelli to give a yip of surprise. Dressed in a flimsy piece of lace and satin, her intent was clear. Had she hoped to climb into his bed? Likely. That's where it would have ended, however.

"Miss Bonatelli, I suggest you return to your bedroom."

"I..."

"Now, Miss Bonatelli."

The girl wilted, transforming from wannabe temptress to the sixteen-year-old girl that she was.

Voluptuous and attractive, sure. Jailbait. off-limits. And her father would kill me if I even think of touching her.

She turned away, her shoulders slumping.

And that would have been the end of it, had not the door at the far end of the hall not opened at that precise moment. In the days that followed, Shane would have time to think about how unlucky he was that Don "The Boss" Bonatelli took that moment in time to go in search of a midnight snack. Don saw his underage daughter walking from Shane's room, dressed as provocatively as the girls in one of his strip clubs. Considering that the amount of cloth covering the girl's body left nothing up to the imagination, and she was his only child, the roar of fury that erupted from Don's throat did not surprise Shane.

"Daddy! No!" Heather screeched in a panic. She reached for him, but he was past her and charging down the hallway toward Shane.

Well, shit.

The old man had three decades on Shane. And he was a client that Shane was supposed to protect. These facts flitted through Shane's mind in the few seconds it took for Don to close the distance and slam into Shane. His meaty ham hock hands slamming home with surprising accuracy. Shane danced back, the door of his room flying open and Don's body hurtled through the open doorway, uncontrolled, as the object of his fury moved nimbly back and swept the older man's legs out from under him.

The floor shook as Don fell, face first, with a loud grunt. This earned a shriek of dismay from Lucia Bonatelli, who was half-asleep, a dark face mask coating her entire face except for her Botox-plump lips and oblong circles for her eyes. Her hair, normally coiffed with care, was a nightmare of frizzy bedhead. She screamed again at the sight of Heather cowering near her door. A scream that turned to a snarl of anger and fury as she realized her daughter was wearing an outfit filched from her, and appeared to be coming from Shane's room. Shane watched as the older woman's eyes narrowed into angry slits, no doubt fueled by a rage that comes from one who feels another younger, nubile version of herself has upstaged her.

Shane groaned. Lucia had been eyeing him like he was a dessert she just had to taste for the past ten days. Anytime her husband Don was out of the room, she sidled up to Shane, batting her mascara-coated lashes in his direction. Now, she was jumping to the same conclusion her husband had, and she was better armed. Her hands clenched as she advanced toward him down the hall, snarling curses. Shane had watched her spend two full hours on the nails on the left hand alone the day before, filing them and painting them blood-red.

Don pushed himself up with a groan from the floor, a growl building in his broad, hairy chest. "You, sonofabitch!"

"Mr. Bonatelli, Mrs. Bonatelli, I need you to both calm down." Shane held out a hand and tried to monitor Lucia's advance as her husband recovered himself enough to rise again. "Miss Bonatelli was out in the hall. I told her to go to her room. Nothing else happened here tonight."

The words spewing from Lucia Bonatelli's mouth were unrepeatable. They called into question his legitimacy, his sexual tastes, and much more. Don Bonatelli was moving slowly, which was good for Shane, but also concerning. This was especially true when the man clutched his left arm and groaned. The light from the hall showed a sudden sheen of sweat across the older man's balding pate.

"I am going to ki..." He collapsed back to the ground, falling on his side before gravity took him onto his back. His pale, hairy, overly blubbered chest rising and falling as he gasped and choked.

Shane wasn't sure what the man planned to do, other than possibly die from cardiac arrest, and by that point Lucia Bonatelli had reached the doorway, still fixated on gouging holes in Shane's face, judging from the angle of her attack. She seemed unaware of the physical distress her husband was currently under, and Shane dodged as she raked her blood-red claws in his direction.

"Mrs. Bonatelli, stop!" He wrestled one hand, then another, raising his voice above her banshee screeches. The air was turning blue from her misuse of coarse language and now Heather, who had gone from cowering against the door to fully panicking at the sight of her father in the doorway, dove past her mother and Shane. Lucia Bonatelli was not the keenest observer. She seemed to think that Heather was returning to be molested further by the perverted bodyguard their family was currently at the mercy of, and flailed and fought, her teeth snapping as she tried every weapon at her disposal to free herself from Shane's grasp.

"Mom, stop! Stop! Daddy's having a heart attack!" Heather wailed at their feet and finally, after two more repetitions in increasing panic, Lucia relented, and turned instead, throwing herself to the ground as she alternated between screaming invectives and trying to hug her husband to death.

"Ma'am, if you could please let me..."

"Donny, wake up! Don't leave me here in this hellhole with this stupida guardia del corpo con un cazzo flosciol! Amore mio, amore mio, torna da me!"

"Mrs. Bonatelli, he needs CPR."

"Vaffanculo, idota! Amore mio! Cosa ti ha fatto questo mostro?"

Christ.

Don Bonatelli, first red-faced, then purple, and now a steady shade of grey, was fading fast. His eyes fixed. Heather was screaming, Lucia crying, with more Italian tripping from her lips. If looks could kill, Shane would writhe on the ground next to Don Bonatelli, his end in sight.

If I don't do something quick, this guy is going to die.

He reached for the girl's arm, shook her, and her scream stopped abruptly. Shane barked at Heather, "Call 9-1-1. Now!" The kid nodded and scrambled to her feet.

"Mrs. Bonatelli, get the fuck off of him *now*." He accompanied his words with a decisive shove, which sent the woman sprawling, her nightgown riding up over her wide hips, her rant momentarily suspended in the shock of being so rudely pushed aside.

Shane knelt by Don Bonatelli's side, laced his fingers together and began chest compressions. The corpulent man under his hands lay still, unmoving. He counted to ten, then administered the breaths, just as they had taught him. Jack, his boss, made it a point to send Shane and the other bodyguards to annual training for it. And for that, Shane was grateful. The training, which he had attended merely a month before, was still fresh in his mind.

His entire focus was on saving the life of the man in front of him. He returned to chest compressions, and Lucia glared at him and pulled her nightgown down over her thighs. Tears dripped down her cheeks as she mumbled what sounded like curses. It was all in Italian, and short of a few words that seemed similar enough to English, he wasn't getting much out of it other than "Die, fucker, die." He couldn't help wondering exactly who Lucia Bonatelli wanted to die. Shane or Lucia's husband?

"They want to know if he has a pulse." Heather's shaky voice interrupted as Shane administered the last of another set of breaths. He returned to chest compressions.

"Just tell them to hurry." He feared stopping for a second the compressions and breaths, but it was already wearing at him. The paramedics could check for a pulse when they got here. "Go unlock the door for them."

Moments later, the fire truck and ambulance arrived, and Shane moved out of their way. He felt wrung out, like a limp noodle as he watched them apply an AED. 3 Seconds later, Don "The Boss" Bonatelli's skin looked far less gray and his chest was rising and falling on its own. His eyes were closed, though, a line of drool escaping his mouth and crusting on the left side.

"Name?" The EMT asked.

"Don Smith." Shane replied, before Lucia or Heather could answer. "I'll bring his wife and daughter in the car."

"The hell you will," Lucia spat, "My Donny needs me." She scooted into the ambulance, her flimsy nightgown ratcheting up one side as she scooted to sit next to her husband's side, a death grip on his hand. She muttered curses under her breath, glaring at Shane.

The EMT looked at her and back at Shane. "Smith, huh?"

Shane nodded, "Yup."

The man's eyes traveled over to Heather, lingering there for a long second before nodding in return. "Okay, then. He's stable for now and we're taking him over to Mercy off of Hemlock Drive."

"See you there," Shane said, his hand on Tiffany's back. He had to get her off of the street. Neighbors were staring. The ambulance drove away, and he gave the kid a light push towards the hall. "Go get dressed and find some clothes for your mom, too."

He retrieved his phone from his room.

Jack is going to love this one.

Heather reappeared a few minutes later, suitably clothed, pale, and cowed. She held her mother's voluminous purse under one arm, and a stack of clothes and shoes close to her chest. Shane pocketed his phone. Arrangements were already being made for a change of guard and location once Don Bonatelli was stable enough to be moved. Among dozens of homes scattered across the country, Shane's boss, Jack Benton, also owned a hospital in Ohio, just a short flight away.

Who the hell owns a hospital, anyway? Shane shook his head at the thought.

"Well, that's not optimal." Jack's only response to Shane's description of the seduction gone wrong and debacle that followed brought a wry smile to Shane's lips.

The understatement of the year.

At least Jack didn't seem pissed. Not at the late hour, nor at Shane's handling of the situation. Which was a relief. He felt as if he had been walking on eggshells for a year now. Shane had promised Jack he would never sleep with a client again after Lila, and he'd meant it, but for a split second as he relayed the story, he'd wondered if Jack would believe him or not. He had, though. Jack had an uncanny way of sussing out the truth. Shane was pretty sure his boss could smell it; kind of like dogs could smell cancer.

He'd felt nothing but relief when Jack said he would send Luke out to take over. The Bonatelli family were a handful, and one he was happy to fob off on someone else.

Shane looked at Heather Bonatelli. Her mascara had left streaks down her rouged cheeks. She looked even younger than her sixteen years and she stared at the ground, unwilling to meet his eyes. "I'll tell Mama and Papa you did nothing."

"I already told them that."

One horny little teenager and his assignment shot to hell. He hadn't so much as looked at her. How had she made the leap to trying to jump in his bed?

"I'm sorry."

"Me too, kid, me too."

"I just..." she licked her lips and cast a quick nervous glance his way. She looked miserable. "I just, you know, all my friends they've all, you know, *done* it. And they think I'm, you know..." She bit her lip and scuffed one shoe along the ground.

Shit. Now I feel bad for her.

"Tiffany. You're never going to see those girls again. It doesn't matter what they think. The next school you go to, when all this shit is behind you and you've got a new name and a new place to live, you can make yourself into whoever you want to be. And they won't know any different. Keep that in mind. Okay?"

She glanced up and he could see the realization dawn in her eyes. Her back straightened, and she blinked. He could tell she was imagining what a future like that could look like.

"Come on, let's get you to the hospital."

1. "Stupid bodyguard with a limp dick! My love, my love, come back to me!"
2. "Fuck you, you idiot! My love! What has this monster done to you?"
3. Automated external defibrillator

Overheard

- Denise-

It had been an amazing day, and Denise couldn't wait to share it. Lionel always called her and invited her over, but this evening she would drop by and surprise him for once. She'd finished her practicum and passed her licensure exam with flying colors. Next step was to find a position!

She had practically floated down the steps from Miami Regional. She was so close, *so* close. Just a few weeks left to go until graduation and she would be a full-fledged professional nurse.

There had been no time to celebrate, however. Just enough time to grab an Enrollada de Pincana from Coloyo's and then hump it to the three blocks over to her shift at Happy Haven. There she'd filled in for Tonya, who normally worked the ice cream shop shift, where the residents would gather in dribs and drabs to order the ice cream cones.

She enjoyed slinging ice cream more than sitting at the front entry. When she posted at the front entry, she had to make sure none of the memory care residents tried to slip past. Their bracelets, coded to block access to the exits of the retirement village, automatically locked the doors. And while that was important for the residents' safety, the door locks often enabled at just the wrong time, and caused logjams at the front. Her job there was to guide the memory care patients back away from the doors without causing them to become upset. Sometimes they were combative, no matter how gentle and kind she was. Handing ice cream cones out was far easier logistically and interpersonally. Everyone smiled.

Denise had high hopes that they would consider her for the five nursing positions they had recently posted. Happy Haven's back half was undergoing a major expansion. In another month, the building would have twice as many openings for new residents.

The place was unique and centered on re-creating a small-town feel for all of its residents, many of whom were in the beginning to moderate stages of Alzheimer's. They accepted a range of residents. Some were perfectly capable of independent living. Others needed more help, and some needed a lot of help. Walking through the halls, or the courtyard, everyone looked happy, content. And more often than not, that was the atmosphere here. And it was certainly what had attracted Denise to staying on here in a more professional role once her studies were complete.

Just a few more weeks!

She handed Mrs. McKenzie a sugar cone with a scoop of strawberry ice cream and rainbow sprinkles on it. The old woman beamed at her, her mouth splitting into a cheerful grin. Mrs. McKenzie said little, thanks to frontotemporal dementia, and Denise brought the ice cream to her seat, so she didn't have to get up. She was unsteady on her feet, slow, but Mr. McKenzie stayed by her side. He smiled at her gratefully. The cherry-chocolate flavor was her favorite, but it was on back order.

"Thank you, Denise."

"Of course, Mr. McKenzie. Do you want your usual?"

"Yes, thank you."

A moment later, she set his cup of hot cocoa in front of him. He spared a glance for her, nodding thanks, but his gnarled hands were busy catching drips of ice cream from his wife's chin.

Denise handed him a stack of napkins and moved on to the next customer, three ladies in red hats cackling away in the corner.

The next few hours passed in a blur. The ice cream shop was a popular destination. Denise scraped the bottom of the sugar-free vanilla container, making sure Mrs. Bird had a full scoop. Like her last name, the woman was thin, petite, with dark eyes in a small face. Her hair was short, cropped close to her head. Mrs. Bird had diabetes; a piece of vital information transmitted by her bracelet. A piece of technology unique to each resident in the retirement village. In cases like the ice cream shop or the scattering of different restaurants and cafeteria, it transmitted a quick reminder of dietary restrictions when the resident walked in. This helped maintain a sense of independence and dignity for those who couldn't make the best of decisions any longer.

Yet another reason I love working here so much.

Cherie, the next girl on duty, waltzed in at half-past three. "Hey girl!" She was a year behind Denise in the same nursing program at Miami Regional. Her bright smile lit up the room and she glanced at the clock on the wall. "Ms. Eckles in HR asked me to come by a little early. She says you have an interview scheduled at four?"

Denise grinned in return, leaned in and whispered, "I think I've got a shot at one of the new nursing positions they're offering." Cherie hugged her.

"I'm rooting for you, girl. How did the licensure exam go?"

"Passed."

"Yes! I knew you would! Just like you'll ace the interview."

Denise hugged her back. "You are a gem!"

Moments later, she sat back straight, fully focused, as the interview began. She had met Oona, the Human Resources director, only in passing when she first interviewed at Happy Haven. Oona handled the medical personnel hires, while Lyda, the assistant director, handled the other positions.

Oona Valere had struck her as cold, and rather distant previously. It had unnerved her. Likely because she was so nervous and wanted the toe into Happy Haven so badly. As a teen, she had enjoyed volunteering at a nursing home and working for one now felt like a natural progression. Especially now that she had her degree. Now she was unnerved again, but in a much different way. Oona was practically purring as she looked over Denise's application and transcripts.

"I see you have scored at the top of your class there at Miami Regional. Impressive."

"Thank you, Ms. Valere. I've, uh, enjoyed my studies."

"Mr. Bush speaks highly of you." And there it was. The reason the Human Resources director was so friendly.

Oh my God, does she know I'm sleeping with him?

"Oh, he does?"

"Yes, he mentioned you by name, said you were just finishing up with your training at Miami Regional." The look on Oona Valere's face was rather inscrutable.

She has to be trying to figure it out. Our connection.

"I likely mentioned it. I see him often at my post in the front."

This was mostly true. After all, that is how they had first met.

Thankfully, it seemed to be enough to satisfy the director's curiosity. "Yes, of course. That makes sense. I gather that is why you began working with us?"

"Yes, ma'am. I volunteered at a nursing home as a teen. It, well, Happy Haven is changing the way we think of aging with dignity. I guess I just really wanted to be a part of that."

Oona smiled. The smile almost reached her eyes.

"That is good to hear, Ms. Fortuna. And yes, Happy Haven's goal is to have more forward-thinking individuals and caregivers who see how different we are, and what we can provide to our residents that no one else has." She tapped her pen over the papers arrayed before her and made a notation. "I think you will be an asset to Happy Haven, Ms. Fortuna. If you can wait for three more months, the new wing will open in August, and that is when we would need your nursing services. This is the starting amount. I expect approximately 15-30 hours of overtime each month may be required as well."

"I graduate next month, so, yes, that is more than acceptable for me, Ms. Valere." Denise's heart soared at the figure written on the page. It was five times the amount she was making. After years of struggle, scrimping, saving, and driving a car old enough to drink, she could see her fortune truly changing. And with a company she could truly enjoy working for. One that was honest and had its residents' best interests at heart.

I can't wait to tell Lionel!

Less than half an hour later, she stood inside of Lionel's glass and steel house, frozen. The exuberance that had driven her to drive to his house, uninvited, unexpected, suddenly draining from her. His voice, it was so different, so cold and business-like.

"No. Not at the Miami location. Too many eyes are on that one. Think backwater, provincial. The lower-income states with the politicians we can manipulate."

There was a pause. "Yes, have Lewis pull up dirt on all of them. We'll only do drug trials on select locations and residents. This is the initial test phase." Another pause. "No, they are still working out the kinks in dosage. We need test subjects with no family or friends. No one to complain if the subject has an adverse reaction."

Denise stood there outside of his home office, hand frozen in midair, about to push the door open. What was Lionel talking about? The tone of his voice sounded completely different from the kind and thoughtful lover who had asked about her family, her childhood.

"Right. Two drugs. We can do more in the lower-income areas." Another pause. "Death rate is right at thirty-eight percent for the Stultuzole, and the Augerezene stands at six percent in primate trials. The clients are fine with the numbers on the Stultuzole, but the Augerezene needs to be under three percent or less if we want to sell it. We test it on the adults, then move into the incarcerated population. I have several pools of test subjects ready and waiting for that stage of human trials."

Denise backed up, her mind whirling. Lionel was talking about drug trials on *humans*. And, considering he was CEO of Happy Haven Retirement Villages, it didn't take much of a leap to realize where those drug trials were happening.

She needed to leave *now*, before he realized she was here.

"Yes, yes, I understand. Rollout for both drug trials has already begun in Hammond and Durant."

Hammond, Louisiana? Durant, Oklahoma? Those were both the two newer Happy Haven Retirement Village locations. Oona Valere had asked her if she had any interest in working in either. Denise had told her no, of course. She loved living in Florida. Perhaps someday she would change her mind. Her roommate Taegan talked endlessly about becoming a traveling nurse. But Denise had her friends, a life here. Or she had.

Whatever I'm hearing. I'm not meant to hear. I need to go. NOW.

Her car. He hadn't heard her come in, but he would hear her trying to leave. The damn thing never started on cue. It took a couple of tries. She turned and eyed the front door she had come in through. She walked quietly, easy to do with tennis shoes. Denise walked up to the door, carefully opening it, only to hear Lionel end the call, his chair creaking as he stood up.

Shit.

She spun on her heel and let the door thump closed behind her. "Hello? Lionel? I have the best news!" Denise forced a broad grin on her face.

When he appeared at his study door, his face closed, tense, she nearly lost her nerve.

"What are you doing here, Denise?"

"I tried your cell, but it went to voice mail and I just couldn't wait to tell you the big news!"

"What news is that?" He asked, closing the distance between them. It unnerved her.

She smiled, likely a little manic in her desperate attempt to look normal. *Nothing to see here other than an excited girlfriend showing up unexpectedly.*

"I passed my licensure exam with flying colors and, even better, I interviewed today and got one of the nursing positions at Happy Haven!"

His face changed back to the gentle lover she remembered. "Congratulations, my dear! We should celebrate!" He hugged her to him and she stiffened in his arms. She wanted to run as far and as fast as she could from this place. She needed to sort this out in her head, maybe talk to one of her friends, and figure it all out first. Lionel seemed so kind, so thoughtful. Had she misheard? Misunderstood? He pulled away and looked down at her. Denise realized he was expecting some kind of response.

"I'm so sorry, I can't." Denise forced her shoulders into a hopefully carefree shrug. "I promised my roommates we would go out. They want to take me out for a celebratory dinner. Perhaps tomorrow?"

"Of course." His dark eyes bored into her, studying her.

"What is it?" Denise asked, doing her best to keep her voice steady.

"Nothing. Just proud of you and your hard work. You will make a fine nurse, Denise."

"Thank you."

She made her excuses and forced herself to stroll out of the door when all she really wanted to do was run. Her car started on the first attempt and Denise drove away, glancing in the rearview mirror as she did. Lionel stood there, unsmiling, watching her leave. Above him was a security camera. How had she never noticed that before?

Help is Hard to Find

- Lila -

Lila stared at the large ornate clock that hung over the front door of the bookstore. Angela was late, later than she had ever been, and Lila's stomach growled in distress. The booming thunder of the incoming summer storm had woken her in the wee hours of the morning. After that, she had fought to return to sleep as her mind immediately revved up and started cycling over the latest plot twist, or lack thereof, on dreaded book number two. The first book had just poured out of her. This one, however, was not that simple.

And thanks to not sleeping, she had then overslept. The sun was blinding as it shoved its way past the thin floral curtains and lit up the room. Cheery sunshine wasn't so nice when you were sleep-deprived. It had taken her a while to return to sleep as the wind and rain lashed the outside of the small rental house. Apparently, this had resulted in a power outage as well. The clock by her bed blinked a steady 12:00 in red, and Lila had cursed under her breath as she reached for her phone and read the time. Her phone's display told her she had less than fifteen minutes before it was time to open the store.

No time for a leisurely breakfast. Not even time for coffee or a quick shower. She had scrambled out of bed, tossed on clean clothes and ran out of the door with her Contigo in one hand and her purse in the other.

Mrs. Danbury had been there, like clockwork, at the door at two minutes past nine. A pleasant smile appeared on her face.

"Good morning, Felicia, I'll take two pork chops, please." Before Lila could answer, the old woman had waved a finger, "Cut thick, mind you. Murray hates thin chops."

Murray, long dead of cancer, had been quite particular about his cuts of meats. Lila had learned this and other odd details about the man from Mrs. Danbury, including that Murray never wore blue, preferred the boxers over briefs and was of the opinion that women, not just children, should be seen but not heard. Lila sighed, "Mrs. Danbury, I don't carry meats. Only books."

The old woman stood at the counter and stared at Lila, confused. "But Murray expects pork chops tonight. It's Wednesday!"

Lila nodded. There was no point in arguing. "I am so sorry, Mrs. Danbury, but we are fresh out of pork chops. However, there's someone else who can likely help with this." She placed a hand on the woman's frail, bony shoulder and guided her toward the glass door. She pointed with her other hand. "There is Hannaford's just down the street. I'll bet you anything they have pork chops."

Mrs. Danbury gazed out of the window glass. She bit down on her lower lip, a look of concern on her face.

"I don't know. Papa said I shouldn't cross a busy street, not with all the cars going past so quick." Her voice sounded younger, higher, less mature.

Okay, it's going to be one of those *days.*

Lila looked around, hoping beyond hope that Mrs. Danbury's grandson would show up soon. She could get the old woman across the street to Hannaford's, but Lila knew she would be back. After all, the building next door to the bookstore had once housed a bakery, and Murray, dead some twenty years or more, had been particular to a certain French bread the bakery, now a decade gone, had baked. She could see that, for now, the street outside was empty of cars. So was the sidewalk in either direction. The tourists weren't up yet, and no customers would show up for an hour, possibly two.

"I'll be happy to walk you across the street."

Mrs. Danbury's face lit up. "Oh, thank you. You are ever so kind!"

Lila scanned the street. No one else was out except the local stray, Sir Riley Brunswick, who everyone fed bits and scraps to. He sauntered down the sidewalk, sniffing the ground near one of the round public trash cans, and then lifted a leg to claim it as his. No sign of Angela. Lila suppressed another sigh. She was hopeless with managing employees and Angela seemed to sense that. She was perennially late, and the past two weeks had been especially bad now that she had fallen in love. Again.

Lila smiled at Mrs. Danbury and placed a hand on the older woman's bony shoulder. "Don't worry, I'll walk with you the entire way." She left the door unlocked. After all, the town was still half asleep, after all. The likelihood that anyone would walk into the bookstore and run off with a wheelbarrow full of books was small. Last night had been the annual Fourth of July celebration and the smell of sulphur still hung heavy in the air. The gathering storm had politely waited until the last of the fireworks lit up the sky before it unleashed a torrent of rain on everyone below. By then, Lila had been comfortably asleep in her bed. She'd watched the fireworks from her large window upstairs earlier and thought of the fireworks shows at home in Kansas City.

Home. Well, it used to be home. She couldn't return. Not for a year or two, possibly never. The lawyers in the WitSec program had hedged around that minor fact like pros. And Lila understood that once you were in, you never got to leave WitSec. At least, not as they continued to dig into the financial records of Kurgen Real Estate. The investigation had broadened and the chance that anything would go to trial was becoming a distant possibility with each month that passed.

"It's like cutting off the head of a hydra," her handler had explained. "This is deeper than we could have possibly imagined." And meanwhile, Lila's life was here. It wasn't a terrible life. Honestly, when she thought about it, living surrounded by books, and now writing her own books, well, it was a life she had dreamed of and wanted more than the data analyst job at Kurgen.

How many times did I hear that becoming a writer wouldn't pay?

They canceled her student loans and other debt as part of her inclusion in WitSec. Technically, they probably still existed, but she had a different last name now, a different social security card, and was in a small town in Maine where the likelihood of anyone from her past life ever running into her was infinitesimally small.

Mrs. Danbury tucked her hand into the crook of Lila's elbow and they walked down the street, crossing slowly at the crosswalk, moving at a leisurely pace. Lila's stomach grumbled again, and she was thankful that the old woman had provided an excuse for her to stop by Hanniford's and get something, anything, to eat.

Who knew how long it would take Angela to show up, after all? She'd mentioned yesterday that she was going out with Kenny, who ran the gift shop down the street. He was the third boy that Angela had fallen for since the school year ended and tourist season began in late May. Each time she did, her attendance worsened. Lila was beginning to believe it would be better to handle the bookstore herself and possibly shorten the hours so she could write in the early morning or in the evening after work.

"Such a lovely day," Mrs. Danbury's voice jostled Lila from her musings. "What month is it?"

Lila steered her around a pile of discarded fireworks tubes. "It's July, Mrs. Danbury. Did you watch the fireworks last night?"

Mrs. Danbury's answer was lost as Joel, her great-grandson, called from the far corner. "There you are, Gran!"

Lila could see from the teen's appearance that he had likely rolled out of bed, dressed and shoved his feet into shoes before he rushed out of the house in search of the old woman. He wore a rumpled shirt, and the buttons didn't align quite right. His tangled dark hair was flat on one side. She could see drool dried on the side of his mouth. He shot a nervous glance at Lila, barely making eye contact.

"I'm so sorry, Miss Brewer."

Even after living as Annie Brewer for more than a year now, Lila still had to remind herself forcefully that it was her name. "I thought I locked the door last night after the fireworks, but I guess I forgot." His eyes darted about, and he focused on his grandmother instead of looking at Lila. She suppressed a smile. She'd caught him staring at her several times over the past few months. Usually, they seemed to center on her breasts, but occasionally his gaze made it to her lips. Each time, he blushed from the bottom of his neck to the roots of his hair. She could see the red creeping up his neck and into his ears. The red made them stand out more than they already did.

"Not a problem, really, it wasn't. It's pretty quiet this time in the morning."

"Michael, darling, I need to get pork chops for your father." Mrs. Danbury was not to be deterred. "You know how he is, so set in his ways!"

"It's okay, Gran. I bought the pork chops last night. They're in the icebox waiting for your special recipe." The young man said.

Mrs. Danbury seemed to accept this and Joel flashed a rare smile towards Lila before ushering his great-grandmother away.

Lila watched them go. Her heart hurt for the two of them, especially Joel. Maeve, the town gossip, had told her that Joel was an orphan. First, his mother died of a drug overdose when he was barely out of diapers, and then his grandfather Michael, Mrs. Danbury's only son, had passed away from a heart attack when Joel was fifteen. After that, it had just been Joel and his great-grandmother alone in the house.

"Michael went and joined his dear wife Heather in heaven, God rest his soul. Heather passed on of leukemia when Joel's mother Natasha was just a little girl," Maeve had said, wiping at a nonexistent tear. "And that sweet young Joel has seen nothing but loss and heartache." Her nose had twitched, "And of course no one knows who his daddy is. It could be anyone, really. Natasha was, well, you know, kind of loose. All the boys in town knew about a certain little strawberry-shaped birthmark on her rear, if you know what I mean."

If there was a drawback to living in a smaller town like Brunswick, it was that gossip seemed alive and well. Lila hated to think about what Maeve might say about her. The Brunswick queen of gossip appeared to have dirt on everyone. Take the owner of Hanniford's, for example. He was a round, slightly balding man of fifty who, if Maeve was to be believed, enjoyed dressing in women's clothes. Once Hanniford's closed and the sun slipped below the horizon, Lyle Cobbler would retire for an evening of dress-up, complete with rather garish makeup. A harmless little secret that was exposed one evening when his toaster went up in flames and caught the kitchen curtains on fire, prompting a visit from the Brunswick Fire Department.

Lila hadn't been able to look at him since without imagining him dressed in stockings and an extra-large blue satin teddy from Frederick's of Hollywood. Maeve was rather detailed in her description. It was after a visit from Maeve that she missed the anonymity of city life the most. Small towns knew everything. She knew Maeve knew all about her love life, or lack thereof. In fact, Lila was sure of it. Hadn't Maeve mentioned, no less than three times, that Lila should go to O'Donoghue's for a bite and a pint, hinting that there was an active singles scene there.

Maybe Maeve is right. Maybe I need to get out and try dating. It's been six months, after all.

Six months of silence. Six months since she had told Shane not to visit anymore. Not after that last disaster. All of her plans, the special romantic escape she had planned, everything, just vaporized because he needed to work. After his boss had given him the time off, only to take it back and say he needed Jack for a job. Damn Jack Benton. If that was the life of a bodyguard, well, it wasn't a life she was comfortable with.

Waiting around for weeks on end for him to show up, and then leave again? How many times did it have to happen before she got the message? Shane's work was his life, not her.

Mind-blowing sex? Check. Sexy as hell? Check. Amazing cook? Check. Pretty much everything I am looking for in a guy? Check. Except he is already married... to his work.

Still, she missed him. She found her thoughts drift to images of him, in her bed, in the shower, in the kitchen. He made the best omelets. Her stomach reminded her yet again that its current emptiness was completely unacceptable.

Nope, the only thing I need is food, not a dating life on top of running a bookstore and starting a writing career. Besides, why give Maeve more gossip? Her cousin runs O'Donoghue's. I'll bet she is in there all the time. Last thing I need is her speculating on my sex life, or telling everyone else how loose I am!

She watched as Joel and Mrs. Danbury disappeared around the corner. She debated whether she should head back to the bookstore. Her stomach twisted in complaint, and she wished she had eaten more than carrots and peanut butter while squeezing in her words for the day last night, even as her energy levels drooped. Angela had called in sick yesterday, and Lila had been on duty nonstop, from open to close, with only enough time to shove a reheated chicken drumstick down her throat in between customers. Today wasn't looking much better. At least yesterday she had woken on time, ate breakfast and packed leftovers in her lunch bag. Today, she had been in too much of a hurry.

With another quick glance up and down the street, she decided, then walked the last few steps to Hanniford's.

Stock up food for the day. Not just a donut or muffin, but lunch as well, and snacks. I'll bet anything that Angela is a no-show.

"Morning, Annie!" Andie waved at her as she walked in. Lila smiled and waved back. Andie was Lyle Cobbler's niece, and ran most of the operations of the small grocery store, stocking the shelves, running the register, cleaning the bathrooms. Lila sighed, wishing she could get lucky and get a girl like Andie to work for her. But the bookstore didn't make enough to pay more than minimum wage, thus she seemed stuck with kids like Angela. Still, she would ask Andie the next time the girl was over browsing the science fiction section if she was interested. At least Andie was interested in books. Angela found books "boring" and Lila couldn't even depend on her to re-shelve the books in alphabetical order.

Spending my days surrounded by books is pretty damn nice. But it would be nicer if I had a little help that I could rely on.

Lila moved through the aisles and collected enough in fruits and pre-made items to get her through the day, including a microwavable meal she could eat for dinner that evening. She was behind, and struggling with the current book project. And if Angela didn't show up for work, Lila would likely have zero time to work on it during the day. Another twenty minutes, maybe less, and the foot traffic would pick up. Then there would be shoppers there to keep her hopping.

"Find everything, okay?" Andie grinned at her.

"I did. Hey, the newest book in that *Gliese 581g* series you like just came in. *G581: Plague Tales*? Come by this afternoon and I'll have it for you." Lila answered. Andie squealed with excitement. The girl inhaled books, and her interests didn't stop at science fiction. She had been one of Lila's beta readers for her first book.

"Oh my God! Yes! I've been waiting for this! I'll be off at three, maybe four."

"Great, I'll see you then, Andie." She leaned close and winked at the girl, "And hey, if he keeps refusing to pay overtime, you can always come and work for me." She whispered.

Andie giggled. "I'd love that so much, but I'd probably spend my entire paycheck on books!"

"Employee discount is 30%!" Lila said and made her escape before Lyle caught her trying to swipe his best employee.

Outside, the heat was rising along with the sun, and she could see half a dozen people, mostly tourists, moving about. Time to get to work.

Leading with the Small Head

- Indalo -

Lionel watched Denise's car drive out of sight before he pulled up the security camera feed. He rewound to the time when her car had arrived. The time stamp showed 6:32 p.m. He watched her get out of it and walk toward the house. He then pulled up his call log. The call ended at 6:35. By then, according to the security feed, Denise had already been in the house for three minutes. He ground his teeth.

Damn shame. She would have made a fine nurse.

He would have to let Beta know. It was protocol in cases like this. It was past midnight there. She often stayed up late, however.

The phone rang once, twice, then clicked.

"I'm busy." The woman's voice was calm. "What could be so important?"

He wet his lips. "I have a situation here."

A small sigh of irritation sounded along with the rustle of bedsheets. He could hear her murmur to someone else. The door creaked open. He even heard the groan of wood under her feet, before she closed the door to her study behind her. He recognized the door as it closed. Nothing sounded quite like a 500-year-old oak door when it closed.

"I thought you were in Marrakesh."

"Change of plans, love, I took a quick detour to Bacharach."

He grimaced. The name of her detour was Wolfgang, age twenty-seven. He was part of an Olympic track team and lived in a cramped apartment a few blocks from the city center. She had brought him to the villa, to the bed they shared, instead of fucking him in his tiny, cramped apartment. His wife loved her creature comforts.

He heard the creak of a chair as she settled into the large armchair in the office. "Well, go on, what is it you need, Lionel?"

"A girl, she overheard something she shouldn't have, and she's in the wind."

Another sigh. "Couldn't keep your fun toy on the side and in the dark, could you?" He could hear the leather chair creak, imagined her leaning back in it. Was she naked? Or wearing a negligee? Lionel licked his lips. He wanted to do terrible, dark things to her. Make her scream with pleasure, and maybe a little pain.

"The problem here, dear Lionel, is that you are leading with the small head. It's why I should be Alpha and you should be Beta, not the other way round." She sighed again. "I'll contact Markus. He's reliable. Does good work. I'm assuming you want it clean? Since you were... close?"

He thought he had managed this dalliance more discreetly. Somehow, some way, she had known all about the girl. He stared at the security feed on his phone. Obviously, she had known. She had the same app on her phone. Lionel felt a snarl forming in his throat. He hated when she was one step ahead of him. As of late, that seemed to be a regular occurrence.

"I don't particularly care. If I remember right, Markus enjoys his work. Especially with fire."

She laughed. "Hm... interesting. Well, give me a minute here."

He could hear her fingers tapping on the keyboard. After a few seconds, the chair creaked again, and she spoke. "Consider it done. Tonight, if I don't miss my guess. I'll have Markus contact you for any extraneous details, as I already have most of the information necessary. Address, roommates, and more."

Of course, she did. They might have an open relationship, but she kept closer tabs on him than he did on her. Far closer. For his wife, everything was a chess move, and she knew well in advance who would win the game.

"I expect you do." He said nothing more on the subject, changing topics instead. "Shall we dine in Madrid next Tuesday?" The key to a successful marriage was keeping things exciting inside and out of the bedchamber. "I made reservations at DiverXO."

She practically purred. "DiverXO? I look forward to it."

If there was anything that Joyce enjoyed more than her muscled, yet vacuous boy toys, it was a Michelin star restaurant, and this one had earned *three*.

Still, he couldn't help but needle her. She wasn't the only one whose currency was information on who was fucking who.

"Oh, and darling? Be sure you don't bring any STDs back from Wolfgang." He hung up the phone without waiting for an answer. It was a cheap shot, and he knew it. What could he say? He was human. Open relationship or not, he didn't like the idea of sharing his wife with another man. Especially someone who ran in circles all day.

He made a note to have one of their men in Europe arrange for an accident. Just a small maiming. Perhaps a car accident that would cause a few broken bones. Or a mugging, yes, a mugging would be best. Make sure that dear Wolfgang found himself unable to run fast any longer.

His wife had played with her little boy toy long enough.

A Couple of Days

- Shane -

Shane's phone vibrated in his pocket as he sat in the hallway across from Don Bonatelli's room. Lucia glared at him, muttering epithets in Italian as she stalked inside, an iron grip on Heather's arm. The kid hadn't resisted or complained, just scuttled alongside her mother into the room. Minors weren't supposed to be there outside of visiting hours, but Lucia Bonatelli was a force no one seemed willing to tangle with, not even the dour by-the-books hospital security officer. He'd tried and Mrs. Bonatelli had shot him a look that would leave most fearing for their lives.

It might have gone differently if Shane hadn't interceded then. Explaining he was private security, a bodyguard, often caused more problems than it solved, but dropping Jack's name and his card usually helped defuse any potential problems. Jack's reach impressed Shane. Even here in the middle of nowhere flyover country.

He had settled himself in a chair outside of the room. It was mostly a window, anyway. He could see all the Bonatelli family from his vantage point. His phone buzzed again, and he slipped it out of his pocket. A text from Luke.

On my way. Flight lands at 1000 and I'll be there by 1100.

Shane checked his watch. It was 0800. Three hours to go, likely less. Luke Hall was a down-to-earth, flannel-wearing, outdoor type. When he wasn't working for Jack, he was usually up at a remote cabin he owned up in Alaska. Where Shane had street smarts from his formative years spent on city streets, Luke knew the woods, hunting, and other survival techniques. Jack Benton employed a wide range of talent, former soldiers, police, even those with survivalist training, and he insisted his men learn multiple disciplines. This meant that Shane had trained Luke in Bokator and Luke had given Shane a crash course in surviving the wilderness. It had not been without its hair-raising moments. The remote area had everything from grizzly to moose, and none of them were friendly.

He was tired, but sleep would wait. The chances that anyone knew they were here were minimal, and Lucia had stuck to the last name of Smith. They were already over 1,500 miles from New Jersey, where the name Bonatelli meant something, but one never knew for sure. Better to stay safe and keep his guard up. The girl trying to sneak into his room had unleashed all kinds of merry hell as it was. Shane wasn't one hundred percent sure that Jack believed him when he swore he hadn't encouraged the kid, but that was probably his guilty conscience talking.

I should have never slept with Lila. No, I should have quit my damn job and stayed *with her.*

The thought of her still stirred complex feelings inside of him. More than lust, although there was plenty of that. It had been six months, and he still dreamed of her. What did that say about him? Was it time to get out of this business? Do something different?

Being a bodyguard is all well and fine, but it isn't an end goal, Ellis, and you know it. But what else is there, really?

He wished he could stop thinking about Lila, but that just didn't seem possible. Not when his dreams remained filled with her, and his days felt empty. He knew exactly when it had all gone wrong. The look on her face when his two-week vacation was cut short. She had arranged for a week of activities, even booked a cabin and arranged for ski rentals at Sugarloaf. Everything had been in place. And then there'd been an emergency client, and Jack had needed him.

Shane had ended the call, looked up, and seen the look of hurt and disappointment on Lila's face. Once again, he had put his work first.

I owe Jack. He took a chance on me when no one else would. I'd be in prison if it weren't for him.

These choices, they all had drawbacks, consequences. They seemed to determine his life, limit it, even when he was trying to do the right thing, or at least the lesser wrong thing. Whether it was choosing to pull out of medical school to take care of his dying mother. Getting entangled with the sister of a head gangbanger of the Asian Boyz or trusting for a second that damned Dave Eggers.

Although if I hadn't had followed Dave Eggers, I'd still be in debt to my eyeballs and living in East L.A. eking out a living. And he might have killed Jack.

Conversely, his decision to choose a billionaire stranger over a childhood friend who sashayed down the wrong path had led him to a job that paid extremely well. It was worthwhile and meaningful more often than not. He might not be the doctor he had dreamed of being, or have a family, but in a few more years, those things could happen.

Not with Lila, though. I fucked that up.

He had boarded a plane, flown away. Off to protect some asshole that had pissed off the wrong person. He had called her. The phone rang and rang until voicemail turned on. "Hi, you've reached Lila, leave a message and maybe I'll return your call!" She sounded all bubbles and tease on the recording, but he knew if she wasn't answering, well, it was because she was angry. Their first argument, short as it was, revolved around her demand that he call Jack back and tell him to find someone else. "You should get a vacation every once in a while. One that he doesn't cut short!"

It hadn't been the first time Shane had disappointed her, but it sure as hell was the last. Two days later, after asking for time to think, his phone had rung.

"I just can't do this, Shane. I just... can't. After everything that has happened, I need..." she had stopped, her voice laden with emotion. "I need *normal*. If that even exists. If it is even something I have a right to expect in this insane world. I want you in my life. But not like this. It just can't work. I want to wake up in the morning and know you are lying there next to me. This can't work any other way."

The words he wanted to say deserted him in that moment. His tongue had felt thick, unwieldy, and he had struggled to respond at all. What was there to say, really? What could he really offer Lila?

Face it, Ellis. If she needs a bodyguard, you are her guy. If she needs a partner in life, well, you have a long way to go before you can give anyone that.

They spoke twice after that. Brief, awkward check-ins. In a moment of weakness a few months ago, he'd flown to Maine. Watched her move about the bookstore, while he felt like some damned stalker in a coffee shop across the street. She'd looked happy. Busy. No new guy in the picture yet, at least not from what he could see, but given time, that would change. A beautiful woman like that, well, a woman like her wouldn't stay single for long, even in a small town like Brunswick, Maine. Back on the job, he would catch himself thinking of her, imagining her meeting someone else, settling down, getting married, having kids.

She deserves happiness. She deserves more than a half-life, a half-assed "Hey babe, I'm here for two weeks, oh, sorry, make that two days. Gotta go save somebody now."

Doctors came and went. Occasionally, Heather scuttled out, avoiding looking his way, her cheeks red with embarrassment. A few minutes later, she'd return with a coffee or bag of donuts, scuttling past as if he didn't exist. Poor kid. He couldn't help feeling sorry for her. It wasn't likely that Lucia was going to let her forget it soon, either.

But it isn't my problem anymore now, is it?

As he was thinking this, a familiar face appeared at the end of the hall. Luke had on his trademark flannel shirt and jeans and a creased paper bag in the other. Shane rose from his seat and met him when he was a few paces from the door.

"Ellis."

"Hall."

Luke's green eyes took in the Bonatelli family. Lucia flashed a scathing glare at the two men, Heather briefly glanced over, red flushing her cheeks once again, and Don Bonatelli was peacefully sleeping. Shane hoped he got some decent rest in the hospital, because once they were back in a safe house, some place outside of the hospital in Ohio that Jack had arranged for them to be transferred to, he really doubted the guy would get a moment of peace from Lucia. From the grim expression on her face, he could see she disapproved of Luke.

This was likely for the best. She wouldn't try to seduce him, and Heather had likely learned her lesson from the disaster of the night before. If everyone was incredibly lucky, that girl wouldn't be trying to emulate her mother for a long while. Long enough for the WitSec program to take over once Bonatelli agreed to exchange testimony for a life in some Podunk nowhere town. He saw divorce looming on the horizon. But it wasn't his problem anymore, so there was that liberating fact.

"Brought you something for the flight back." Luke handed him the paper bag and a ring of keys. "Keys to the cabin and the truck. Take it easy around the last bend, will you? The runoff's made the going that way a little dicey. Jack says to check your email for the tickets."

"Will do."

Luke looked over at the Bonatelli's and whistled under his breath as Lucia glowered back at him. "Damn, she looks *pissed*."

"That's just her resting bitch face." Shane said, turning away, just in case Lucia Bonatelli could read lips.

Luke snorted. "I need you to take care of something while you're there."

Shane arched an eyebrow. "Oh? Besides that cord of wood you were hoping I'd chop for you?"

"I got something in a kennel on the back porch. Her name is Sue."

"I'm guessing this isn't a dog." Shane had seen Luke's affinity with wildlife. The last time he'd visited the log cabin Hall had built with his own hands, a three-legged skunk had walked up onto the porch, curled up on a cushion, and taken a nap as if it didn't have a care in the world. The smell had been... overwhelming.

"Black bear cub. About six months old. Mother was killed by poachers shooting out of season. I've got him on a mix of kitten formula and kibble. It'll be feeding time by the time you get back there."

Shane shook his head. "Of course it will." He laughed, then asked. "How's the skunk taking it?"

"Pepe is pissed. Took one look at that bear cub and huffed on out of there tout suite. Haven't seen him in three days."

"Well, I hate to say it, but this domestic situation is far more fraught than frontier land." Shane said, angling a thumb in the Bonatelli family's direction.

"Yeah, Jack filled me in. I think he's still pissed at you over the Benoit job."

Shane groaned. "I'll never live that down, will I?"

Luke grinned. "Probably not. Hey, if you get bored, the fence along the back forty is needing some repairs."

Shane flapped his hand at him and sniffed the bag. "Fry bread? From Tapeesa?" It smelled delicious.

"Of course." Luke grinned as Shane took a large bite. "I think she's really into you."

Pieces of fry bread flew out of his mouth as Shane choked. Tapeesa was a solid three bills and mother of nine children, ranging in age from eight years to the eldest son, who was in his early 20s.

Luke slapped him on the back. "She told me to tell you to come by. They're slaughtering a yak on Thursday night. Help 'em out and she'll send you home with some reindeer sausage and those tasty yak-a-dillas. Their herd is doing real well."

Shane was wondering if he was better off with the Bonatelli family. Luke was probably yanking his chain, but he had seen Luke's Inuit neighbor wink at him several times. He'd chalked it up to a cultural difference, but maybe it meant something far different.

It's a whole different world up there. Wildlife running amok, lascivious, middle-aged women, and a hell of a lot more work than I was hoping for while I get a few days off.

He looked over and saw Lucia glaring at him.

If looks could kill, damned if I wouldn't have the most excruciating death right now.

"Well, I guess I better get going. You'll probably be better off without me introducing you. They should be ready to transport later this afternoon to the Ohio hospital. Good luck, man."

"Hey, you too. And give Tapeesa a hug from me."

"Ha! Nice try, Hall. I'll leave that to you," Shane said as he walked away. After these past few weeks dealing with closed doors, and Lucia's oppressive perfume, he was looking forward to the fresh Alaskan air, even if it included wildlife husbandry, yak slaughter, and fence repair.

Torched

- Denise -

Minutes after arriving home, Tara's tear-stained face at the door pushed Denise's troubles to the back of her mind. Her best friend's left eye was already swelling and darkening. Her lip trembled and her mouth opened, but no sound came out, just more gut-wrenching sobs.

"Tara? Oh my God, sweetie, come inside now."

Laura and Taegan, both in the living room, looked first alarmed, then resigned, to see Tara. It wasn't the first time, and unfortunately, it wouldn't be the last. At least, Taegan had said it three weeks ago, when Tara had spent two days at the condo, nursing a black eye and swollen mouth from a tangle with her mercurial boyfriend.

"Eddie is a piece of shit, Tara. The sooner you dump his sorry ass, the better. Or you'll end up regretting it someday."

Tara vacillated wildly on this, unfortunately. At the moment, sore, and safe surrounded by strong women, she had agreed that yes, her boyfriend was a piece of shit. That had all changed two days later with the onslaught of chocolate, flowers, a card begging her to forgive him, and the biggest, dorkiest stuffed bear Denise had ever seen occupying their front stoop. Tara had gone back.

"Oh, let me guess." Taegan drawled, "Mr. Wonderful turned into a piece of shit again."

"Taegan, you aren't helping." Denise hissed as she helped Tara to the couch. Her friend collapsed in a sobbing, moist heap. Her long hair was limp, bedraggled. Outside, the quick and unexpected summer rain shower had all but disappeared. From the look of it, Tara had been out in the thick of it.

Walked the entire way, no doubt.

Laura was a touch more sympathetic. She got up, filled a plastic bag with ice and offered it to Tara, along with a small reassuring pat on the shoulder. "Here, sweetie, take this." She rolled her eyes at Denise and shook her head. It was clear to Denise that Laura knew, just as Denise did, how it would go. Tara would return to Eddie. Whether it was tomorrow or three days from now, it didn't matter. She'd go back.

Denise had volunteered at a women's shelter in her late teens as part of the community service required by her college program. She'd seen how the cycle continued over and over, until either a woman had finally had enough, or her partner killed her. She'd seen it, held hands with countless women, and seen them swear up and down they were done, just to return.

"I'm so done with him, Denise. I swear to God, I am." Tara sniffled, her voice warbled through the snot and tears. "He hit me because I didn't make the spaghetti the way he wanted it. I couldn't find the powdered Parmesan he likes at the store, just the fresh stuff, and I assumed, I mean, I'm so *stupid*, I thought it would be okay, y'know? I mean, it's *fresh*. Who doesn't like fresh Parmesan?"

"Piece of shit." Taegan said, softening. "Who the fuck likes that powdered crap when you can have fresh?"

Tara looked up at her, a grateful half-smile on her face. It lasted for half a second before it crumpled back into misery. "Then he hit me. Told me I was useless and incapable of following basic instructions."

"Girl, that man is a dick." Taegan said, plopping down on one side of Tara and wrapping a brightly tattooed arm around her.

"Who the hell likes powdered Parmesan?" Laura asked as she headed for the kitchen. "This is gonna take a bottle of wine and some of my famous straight-from-the-package gourmet ramen."

"Tell you what, we'll go kick him in the dick and then cover it with powdered Parmesan." Denise promised not to be outdone by her roommates.

Tara giggled at the last one.

With a tall glass of wine, the ice pack, and the trio's insistence she took part in several rounds of Cards Against Humanity, Tara's tears dried and she laughed along with the others. Denise wished for the umpteenth time that her best friend hadn't fallen madly in love with a complete dick and had instead moved in with her when she had first found the place two years earlier. Tara hadn't, though. And hours later, long after midnight, Tara had succumbed to a deep, wine-heavy slumber in Denise's double bed while Denise tossed and turned.

Perhaps it was the whole weird conversation she had overheard Lionel have, or that she knew with no doubt that Tara would return to Eddie *again* despite everything, or that her body just felt weird and *off* for some strange reason she couldn't quite identify - but finally Denise eased her way out of the double bed. Tara didn't wake as she moved about the room and gathered her shoes, purse, and keys.

Cookies and ice cream.

Life always felt better with a delicious Brookie cookie from Night Owl dipped in a pint of Haagen-Dazs. She would bring a Dirty Diana cookie back for Tara. They were her favorite. Denise peered at her phone. It was just past one. She had plenty of time to walk there, to the grocery store, and then even a quick jog along the beach. By the door to her bedroom, Denise paused.

I should wake her up. Have Tara come with me? We haven't been to Night Owl in forever.

It had been their thing, cookies and ice cream, still tipsy from a night out dancing and flirting with hot guys. But then Tara had met

Eddie. And for a girl who liked her boy of the month, Tara had fallen hard for the *wrong* guy. Her friend was out cold. Snoring, even. Denise shook her head, pulled a sheet over Tara, and closed the door gently behind her. She slipped out of the front door and headed down the street.

Two hours later, she stood gaping in horror, lost among the crowd of onlookers. Her home was a burned ruin. While she had gorged herself on ice cream and cookies, dug her feet into the sand and stared up at the starlit night, her roommates, her *best friend*, had perished.

The flames were mostly gone, but the smoke still billowed. Denise stood there, shock holding her in place, lost in the crowd of spectators and gawkers. The police had established a perimeter and various uniformed men stood inside of it, far enough away that she had to strain to hear them. She couldn't hear all that they said. Just random bits of words.

"Blunt-force trauma."

"Arson."

"No survivors."

"Use of accelerant."

"Intentional."

Her mind cycled, taking the words in. Watched as the bodies, all three of them, came out. Covered, wrapped in body bags, she didn't know which was which, but she knew this. Tara, Laura, and Taegan were all dead. All of them.

Had Eddie done this? No. He was a complete shit, but he knew Tara would be back. It was a cycle they had played out over and over these past two years. Besides, Eddie didn't have the balls to kill Tara and two other girls. He was more of the small-minded bully.

Suddenly Denise couldn't breathe. The conversation she had overheard. The one that had made her uneasy, made the questions come up. Lionel. It had to be Lionel. It had to be. There had been something in his eyes. Something in the way he had asked if she had just come in. She'd lied then, in that moment. She'd smiled at him, told him she'd just come by to tell him the news, and that she had to go. A bullshit excuse. She thought she'd been convincing enough, but now she wasn't so sure. What if he hadn't bought it? What if he had called someone to make one foolish girl go the hell away?

From the back of the crowd came a wild, keening scream. Denise turned to see Tara's boyfriend, Eddie, staring at the house, his eyes black holes of panic and fear. "Tara! Tara!" He pushed forward, shoving several bystanders out of his way, edging closer to her. He didn't notice Denise until he was almost on top of her. "Denise? Oh God, thank God! Where's Tara?"

She tried to make her mouth work. She opened her mouth, closed it, and shook her head, staring back at the coroner's van where they were loading the first of the bodies. Eddie's hands were on her shoulders, shaking her, screaming, then pushing her away as he dove forward through the perimeter, bellowing Tara's name. She watched as the police converged on him, first trying to slow him down, and when he fought, subduing him. The last Denise saw of Eddie Vasquez was of his face, wordlessly screaming through the glass of a police car window at her as they drove him away.

The gawping bystanders stared at her with open curiosity. No one approached her. No one said anything to her, but she could hear their murmurs. Snatches of words, phrases. The rushing in her ears, the sounds of the water, the sirens and machines, all the other noise blocked out most of what her neighbors were saying.

The smell finally caused her to flee. The house had been old, one of the older ones in the area. But as they had brought the bodies out, there had been a different smell, one that turned her stomach, one that was part burned beef, mingled with the stench of burned hair, an almost metallic tinge, and, her stomach roiled, the taste of coagulated blood as an errant breeze struck at just the right moment. It smelled of horror. Of things unmentionable and unnamed. Denise lost all thought as she saw the last of the bodies pulled out of the smoking, shambling remnants of her home. She turned on her heel and ran. Her path was without direction, and it was pure luck that it took her toward her car. She had arrived later than her normal time that evening and missed out on the premium parking in front of the house that she usually managed. Laura had ribbed her about it when she first arrived home. It was a running competition between them.

Oh God. Laura.

Laura's car sat half-melted in the drive. The mint green finish of her Volkswagen Bug was blackened, the paint blistered. Denise fumbled for her keys, hearing them jingle as she dug into the Kate Spade purse Tara had given her for her last birthday. Her hands shook so hard, she felt like a resident at Happy Haven. It took three tries before she could hold them still long enough to get the key to unlock the door and slip inside of the car. The inside of the car was quiet, the air blessedly free of smoke, of that other terrible smell. She slipped inside, closed the door, and for reasons she didn't completely understand, locked the door.

To the left, toward the beach, the dark of night was giving way to dawn. The starlit black sky she had walked under just an hour ago was now gray, and she could see a glow appear at the edge of the horizon.

Tara. Taegan. Laura.

Whoever had done this. Had they thought Tara was her? Sleeping in her bed, and at the quickest of glances, same height, same hair. Her best friends in the entire world had been in that house.

And now they are all dead.

Still reeling, Denise felt her stomach roil again. She fumbled with the door lock and opened the door just in time, throwing up the cookie and ice cream along with the remains of the wine and ramen that Taegan had served up. The combination was revolting, soured with stomach acids. In a daze, she closed the door, reached for a napkin from the glove box, and wiped her mouth. Her keys lay in the seat beside her and she stared at them, thought of the smoking ruin behind her, and picked them up. Mechanically, she slipped on her seatbelt, turned the keys in the ignition, and maneuvered the battered car out of its position against the curve. Her thoughts were a maelstrom of grief, horror, and fear. She made her way to I-95 and then north. Denise did not know where she was going. No thought of what happened next. She just drove. To the east, the sun continued to rise.

In Transit

- Denise -

By the time Denise made it to just south of Jacksonville, it was past noon. The tank was nearly empty; the sun was high in the sky, and her throat parched.

Denise pulled into a Flying J. She filled the tank, then stepped inside of the station. Grabbing water, chips, and a cell phone charger.

I need to eat.

She could see an Arby's, but the thought of meat reminded her of the terrible smell and her stomach twisted again. She dodged a pack of gabbling teens dressed in beach gear and headed for the Cinnabon counter.

"WhatcanIgitcha?"

Denise blinked at the older woman behind the counter. "What?"

"What can I get ya?" the clerk said slower, her eyes scrutinizing her.

"Um, one of those, please." She pointed to the pastries warm on the display rack.

"Halfoffifyoubuytwo." The clerk said, then said again, slower, when Denise gaped at her. "Half off if you buy two."

Denise didn't answer. Just a nod. One. Two. Did it matter? Did anything matter? There was nothing left. Nothing but ash and that terrible smell still in her nose.

The cashier handed her a bag and receipt with her card and she headed outside into the hot Florida sun and swampy, humid heat when the image on a large tv screen overhead stopped her in her tracks. There were the smoking ruins of her house. A banner marched along the bottom of the screen: *Miami Fire Horror - Three Women Found Bludgeoned and Burned in Beach House. Boyfriend of Woman Arrested.*

Denise's hands shook.

They think Eddie did it?

She stood rooted to the spot, her eyes glued to the screen.

Eddie looked absolutely panicked. There's shit you can make up, pretend, and there's stuff that's genuine.

She forced her feet to move. To walk through the doors and outside. The moist heat surrounded her, sucking her energy, what little she had of it, and she sagged under the weight of it, her shoulders drooping. Inside of the car, once the engine was purring and the air conditioning flowing, Denise tried to order her thoughts.

What do I do now?

The down-to-earth part of her was trying to reason it all through. To make sense of it. Had it really been Eddie? If so, perhaps she should return home. Well, not home. Home was gone. But back to Miami, to the police, perhaps.

Eddie didn't act guilty. He looked positively terrified. Worried. Yes, Eddie was an abusive prick. But some part of him cared for Tara, had to, to act that way.

A honk sounded. A car, waiting for her to pull out. The driver held up his hands impatiently. Denise realized the parking lot was full, and she was just sitting in an idling car. She had to do something, had to go somewhere.

Decide, damn it. And make it now.

She pulled out of the parking space and the waiting car slid into her vacated place before she was ten feet away. Denise did not know where to go, but it seemed her hands did. They guided the car back to I-95 North. Headed away, up the east coast. Away from the fire, away from the terrible memories of just a few hours before.

She struggled with what to do next. Her friends were dead. Her home, and every possession she had in the world, burned to ash.

She thought of her mother, Janine. On the day of Denise's eighteenth birthday, Janine had given their landlord a thirty day notice. It wasn't completely without warning. She had long spoken of taking what little savings she had and heading for Europe. "I got pregnant a month into my gap year," she was fond of saying, "And that was that. My life of wandering was over. As soon as you are grown, darling, I'm spending the rest of my life as a gypsy."

That was just what Janine did. By the end of the month, she had sold or given away every possession she owned and bought a one-way ticket to Italy, leaving Denise to figure out what she wanted to do with her life in a tiny rented room that smelled like sour milk. The paper-thin walls broadcast every grumble, snipe or argument of the couple who she rented from. What little support system or security blanket Janine's presence had provided during Denise's formative years fell away. It had taken Denise a year or two of floundering, moving from one unsettling situation to another, couch surfing, and rundown rooms for rent before she stumbled into an interest in the medical field. She had worked in a hospital cafeteria, and that, combined with her excellent grades in high school, had eventually led to enrolling in a nursing program.

Janine checked in every so often. Denise had gotten a text from her mother a week or two ago. She had sent a picture of the bluest water Denise had ever seen and written, "Wish you were here. The Aegean sea is a thing of beauty. Don't forget, it's the cradle of civilization. The stories it could tell!"

Denise had stared at it, returning to it over and over. The words her mother had typed were irritating, like a tag on a shirt, poking at her, scratching.

She doesn't wish I was there. Not the slightest bit. She's happy to be done with the mother's role.

It still hurt a bit. Denise felt as if it had denied her something vital. She saw how her friends lived. Sure, plenty of them had both parents working outside of the home, but their parents still were involved and active parts in their lives. They attended soccer games, helped with bake sales, drove them to Girl Scouts. Her mother had never baked cupcakes, never played the domestic goddess. There had been few rules or boundaries, and Janine had never expected her to call her Mother. Men had come and gone. Janine was a butterfly, never content to settle down. Denise wanted something different. She wanted a career. Someday, she wanted to settle down, get married, and have kids. She wanted to walk into a house and know she owned it. Not some jerk who wouldn't bother to fix the dishwasher or replace the shingles that were falling off the roof.

Denise quickly learned to save every penny she could. Which wasn't much, honestly, but she knew she had at least a thousand dollars in the account. And that, along with a growing and undefined terror of returning to Miami, spurred her north. By the time she reached the outskirts of Philadelphia and visited an ATM, she had a hazy notion of what to do next. Perhaps it was the thought of her mother that made Denise remember a childhood trip to Maine. They had gone there to visit friends, well, friends of Janine's parents, and the people who had raised Janine during her early teens. To Denise's inexperienced eyes, the couple had been ancient. They were both in their late 70s, and Charles, or Uncle Chuck as Denise had known him as, ran a bookstore. His wife, Deidre, who Denise had called Aunt DeeDee, had run a knitting supply shop next door to it. It was the one, and only, time that Janine had tried to shirk her responsibilities as a mother. She had dropped six-year-old Denise off and disappeared for nine months, reappearing only after Deidre had grown too ill to work or care for a small child. It wasn't more than a year or two later that Deidre passed away from cancer and left Charles alone to care for the bookstore and their five-room cottage a few blocks away.

When Denise dreamed of a home, it was invariably of that house. She remembered the smell of the sea, the hot summer she spent playing on the beach, or skulking through the stacks of books and curling up in a corner to read. She wondered if Charles was alive still. Likely not. It had been nearly twenty years.

Still, she pointed the car north, drawn magnetically to the last place she had ever truly felt at peace. The memories of salt and fish and seagulls were still as fresh in her mind as if she had experienced them yesterday. Denise continued to drive, pulling into rest stops and sleeping in her car when sleep became necessary.

Suspect

- Miami Police Department -

"What have you got, Ames?" Jim Sievers asked, his hands desperate for something to do now that he'd been without cigarettes for four days. He reached for the stress ball his wife had given him and squeezed it.

Troy Ames was heavyset, balding, and the man wore a perpetual frown. This wasn't atypical, not in their line of work.

"Swears he didn't do it. Spent half the interview blubbering into a box of Kleenex." Ames answered, tipping back in his chair. The beleaguered piece of furniture groaned in protest.

"Huh." Jim leaned over and retrieved Eddie Lamar's rap sheet. "Domestic dispute. Stalking. Assault. Another domestic dispute. Protection order dismissed a week after issuance."

"Yeah, yeah, I know. The kid is a piece of shit. Loses his temper, hits women. You know, just the kind I tell my girls to avoid dating." Ames frowned deeper, shook his head.

"But?"

"But, what?"

"Aw, come on, Ames, out with it. You don't frown like that when you've nailed the bad guy dead to rights."

Ames snorted. A ghost of a smile flickered across his face. He sat forward abruptly; the chair groaning again. "Eddie doesn't have it in him. And he swears up and down his woman was in the building that burned."

"So?"

"So, that'd make four bodies, not three."

Jim shuffled through the folder on his desk. "We got a Taegan Mc-Masters, age 23."

"Yeah, and a Laura McCoy, also age 23."

"And then a Denise Fortuna, age 22. Those are all the girls listed on the lease and it was a three-bedroom house. What's his girlfriend's name?"

"Tara Weatherby, age 22."

"So, how was this guy picked up?"

"He came in like a locomotive there at the scene. Hot as hell, half off his head, screaming for his girl Tara, and took a swing at an officer. They put him on ice and fingered him for the job. I just, I don't buy it, Jim."

"No chance that this Tara girl up and ran?" Jim asked.

Ames shrugged. "They're identifying the bodies now. Burned to a crisp all of them, but they were dead before that."

Jim raised an eyebrow. "Oh?"

"M.E.'s first look, off the record, is that someone walked inside, bashed the brains out of each of the girls while they slept, then used a can of gasoline to soak the carpet and set the place ablaze. Found the melted can."

"Blunt force trauma. Someone has to be powerfully angry to do something like that. And you don't think this Eddie Lamar did it?"

"He was blubbering like a pansy-assed baby. When I showed him pictures of the scene, he tossed his cookies. All over the damned inter-view room floor. Still smells in there. Lamar's definitely got anger issues, but murder? I don't see it, Jim."

"How soon until we get names on all the victims?"

"Any time now." Ames shot him a rare grin. "You're running later than usual, Sievers. I guess that means you're buying me lunch since I covered for your ass and said you were running down a lead when Sarge asked after you."

Jim nodded. "Taco Bile for lunch then."

"Oh, hell no, brother! You are getting me Taco Negro!"

Jim opened his mouth to argue, but the phone on their shared desk rang at that very moment.

Ames grabbed it. "Detective Ames speaking." He nodded, grunted, and scribbled on a notepad. "Right, thanks, man." He slid the paper over to Jim. "They identified the bodies. We got Taegan McMasters, Laura McCoy, and…"

"Tara Weatherby, Eddie Lamar's girl," Jim finished. "So where is Denise Fortuna?"

"That's the million dollar question, isn't it?" Ames tapped the pen on his desk and frowned. "Girl's roommates and friend bludgeoned to death and set on fire. You'd think she'd be in giving a statement to us at the very least. Maybe she was at her boyfriend's house?"

"Or is it something more?" Jim asked.

"Like what?"

"Shit, I don't know. It's Miami. She could've been running drugs or other dirty dealings. Hell, she could've done this to the girls herself."

"Blunt force trauma?" Ames turned to his computer and tapped a few keys. Denise's driver's license photo and details appeared. "This little girl? I don't see it, man."

"All I'm saying is we track it down, see where it leads. What do we know about this Denise, and the others?"

Ames returned to his computer, and Jim powered his laptop up as well. "You take those first two names. I'll look up the other two."

A half hour later, they had a clear yet perplexing picture. All four girls were medical students at Miami Regional University. All of them had squeaky clean records, except for Taegan, whose record showed they had collared her for underage drinking two years prior.

"They've rented this property for the past two years, no complaints or proceedings from the landlord." Ames mused. "No reason for them to be killed like this. Eddie Lamar is still looking like the prime suspect, but I'm telling you Sievers, it wasn't him. Boy hasn't got it in him. He's a small-minded bully. A control freak, sure, but not a murderer and arsonist."

"I believe you, man. But what else do we have? Some rando who just chooses this house and these girls? And if so, where is the Fortuna girl?"

"We have got to issue a bulletin. Put her name and face out there and get her to come in. Then we can sort this out," Ames said and ran his fingers back across his keyboard. "I'll put in the request to the Sarge, along with my interrogation of Lamar."

"Right. Well, hurry then. I didn't eat breakfast. I figure we can get an early start on lunch at Taco Bile."

"You mean Taco Negro, or I might let it slip to Sarge you overslept again."

Jim laughed. "Fine, fine, you old bastard. Taco Negro it is. Now get to typing."

Later that day, they released Eddie Lamar with a court summons for assaulting a police officer.

They issued a police bulletin on all local news websites and radio stations informing the public that the police considered Denise Fortuna a person of interest in the Miami Beach fire. It asked for information from anyone on her whereabouts.

Two rather dangerous individuals took notice of this bulletin. A man by the name of Markus, who was pissed off as all hell that they had given him insufficient information on his target, and Lionel Bush, who never enjoyed paying money to someone for a job left half-done. Neither were men to be trifled with.

Just for Now

Despite the beautiful weather, the morning had been rather quiet. That had changed in late morning, as tourists filled the sidewalks and made their way down the street. A gaggle of pre-teens were giggling over in the romance section. One, a mousy-looking girl with braces, had spots of color on her cheeks as one of her friends showed her a racy, bare-chested vampire looking to make a meal of the scantily clad woman in his arms. Another of the girls caught Lila watching, and whispered to her friends. They skulked away. Well, as much as a gaggle of girls like that can. Half strut, half awkward stumble, they fled for the section just beyond it that held a plethora of ghost stories that were more appropriate for their age.

Andie had slipped over on her lunch break and was running a finger along the spines of the new releases in the fantasy section, and a leggy brunette was currently perusing the magazines, her perfectly manicured fingers fluttering as they tried to choose between The Knot and Bride's Magazine. A rather large diamond solitaire ring on her left finger caught the sunlight that filtered in through the large floor to ceiling windows.

The bell at the top of the door jingled softly, and a young woman entered. She was a thin, mousy-haired slip of a girl. Lila watched her surreptitiously. She looked exhausted, but also her face had a familiar look on it. Lila had been running the bookstore long enough to recognize it. The look of someone who finds books a solace, and book-stores as a place of renewal and safety. She watched as the young woman moved to run her fingers along the women's fiction, then over to the poetry section, before stopping in front of the bulletin board. A draw for the teens, patrons posted everything from lost and found items to help wanted or services offered on it. It was how Lila had first hired Angela. The girl had seemed like a real go-getter at the onset. Until she fell in love. Now all she wanted to do was snuggle with her boyfriend and call in sick. Lila had fielded the fourth "I'm sick" call in a row yesterday, agreed to her showing up for a half day today and resolved to fire her later in the evening, after closing, if she didn't come through. A shot of despair rolled through her.

I hate firing her. But she's been gone more than she's been here. This is ridiculous.

"Good morning," Lila said, smiling at the young woman. "Is there anything I can help you find?"

The woman looked up, managed a small smile in return, and walked over. Now that she was closer, Lila could see she was actually closer to her mid-20s, likely the same age as Lila, or close enough.

"Oh, hi. Do you work here?" The young woman asked.

"Sure do."

"Do you know if, um, the bookstore is hiring at all?"

Lila looked her up and down. She looked normal, really, and maybe a little old for minimum wage work in a bookstore, but there was something about her. Something the woman was trying very hard to hide.

Fear.

Lila knew what it was like to be afraid.

"It is. It's minimum wage, though. If you are okay with that, I can get you an application. Are you new to the area?"

The young woman nodded. Conflicting emotions played across her face. The door chimed again, and the woman flinched in response, her eyes flitting to the door. Lila handed the application over, along with a pen. "Here, you can fill it out while I take care of this customer."

Half an hour later, and a dozen customers in and out, and the young woman returned. Lila had barely had a moment to breathe, but she had stolen a couple of glances over at the woman as she sat in an armchair and filled out the form. She had tucked her shoulder-length hair back behind her ears and was chewing on her lower lip nervously.

"You look like you could really use another clerk."

Lila's stomach growled audibly. She winced. "That obvious, huh?"

Her phone chimed, and she glanced at it. A text from Angela, claiming her *cat* was now sick, and she had to take it to a vet. The girl couldn't keep her stories straight to save her life. Last week, when she had called in, she told Lila that Pumpkin died that morning and she needed to bury the ancient creature. Now it had suddenly revived itself from the dead and desperately needed a vet? She'd call her tonight and tell her not to bother coming back. The girl would be happier working at one of the dozen restaurants along the pier. She'd find herself a well-heeled tourist boyfriend at the beginning of each week.

Like a Baskin-Robbins of boyfriends. A new flavor every week.

Lila studied the application, noting her recent employment at a Happy Haven Retirement Village. In Florida, no less. What in the world was the girl doing here in Maine? "So, Denise, I see you were in Florida until just recently?" She looked up and met Denise's gaze, waiting for her to speak.

"I, um, was in a relationship and it, um, it didn't work out. It's..." Denise stared at her shoes. "I just... I need to figure some stuff out. I'm a hard worker, and I've got retail experience. And while I never worked in a bookstore before, I really, *really* love books." She added it in a quick rush, as if afraid Lila would boot her out of the door.

There was something terribly wrong. Lila wasn't sure how she could tell, but she could, deep in her bones. The girl was scared, and she was hiding something. What, Lila wasn't sure, but it didn't feel like Denise was trying to mislead her, more that she was scared, truly, deeply afraid.

Lila felt her stomach growl again. She had woken up late again this morning, after having a burst of inspiration that had her typing away on her computer until nearly two in the morning. A sandwich from the deli counter at Hanniford's, one made with rare roast beef and swiss cheese with that spicy mustard, was what she was yearning for in that moment. Her mouth watered at the thought.

Her focus returned to Denise. The girl was frightened, and she looked rather sleep-deprived. From the application, Lila could see that, until two days ago, Denise lived, worked and attended nursing school in Florida. Now she was here, some, what, 1,500 miles away from home? There was a story here. And likely someone who needed help.

She might just be here a day or two. Why not? It isn't as if I have anyone else to depend on. Besides, I want to know why she looks so damn scared.

"Can you start today?"

Denise's eyes widened in surprise. "Um, sure."

"How about this minute?"

Denise blinked. "Okay."

"Great." Lila dug into her pocket and pulled out a twenty-dollar bill. "I need you to run down to Hanniford's and buy us lunch. Tell Andie that Annie would like her regular sandwich. She'll know what I mean. Order yourself something, too. After we eat, I'll show you the ropes."

Denise's mouth opened and closed, and she stood there motionless for a half-second, the twenty-dollar bill in her hand. "Um, okay, I'll be right back." She slipped out the door of the bookstore and the bell gave a soft jingle as she did.

"She's not from around here." Maeve appeared before her, the latest beach read clutched in her hands. Lila blinked. Trust Maeve to walk in without Lila noticing and already want the lowdown on the new employee. If that's what Denise truly was.

Lila forced a bright smile on her face. "Why good afternoon, Maeve! How are you today?"

The busybody peered down the street, watching Denise slip inside of Hanniford's. The older woman gave a small harrumph of disapproval.

"Just this today, Maeve? I don't know if you saw it, but a new book by Shelby Van Pelt just came in. *Remarkably Bright Creatures.* It's supposed to be very good."

Maeve's gaze returned to Lila, and she frowned. "Did you actually hire that girl? Where's Angela?"

"Yes, Maeve, I hired her. And Angela isn't here, unfortunately."

Maeve snorted, "That girl has a flavor of the day boyfriend. Just as loose as…"

"That will be $16.49." Lila interrupted.

Maeve's frown deepened. She wasn't used to being interrupted or ignored. Lila suppressed a sigh. No doubt Maeve would note Lila's behavior as surly and the other denizens of the town warned away by the old cow. Lila tried to think of a compliment while the town gossip fished in her purse for cash. Maeve was one of a handful of holdouts. Most of Lila's transactions were with credit or debit cards.

"Your hair looks quite nice today, Maeve." The woman's surly expression wavered. If there was anything Maeve appreciated more than a juicy piece of gossip, it was someone noticing her appearance. Despite living in a small town, and there being really nothing to dress up for now that she was retired, Maeve inevitably appeared in classic outfits with nary a hair out of place, rings and jewelery just right, and her nails impeccably manicured.

"Oh, thank you, Annie. Here, and," she glanced over to the bookshelf at the new book by Shelby Van Pelt. "Be a dear and set that aside for me? I'll come by once I've finished this."

"Of course." Lila calculated it in her head. Maeve read at a pretty good clip in the winter. Summers, however, meant more social events. Bingo, book club, bridge. She figured she had at least three days of respite, perhaps four if she were lucky, until Maeve returned for her next book and the inevitable dose of gossip. She breathed a quiet sigh of relief as the woman left. Maeve wasn't malicious per se, just petty and intrusive more than anything else. The woman rubbed her wrong, though. And until Lila knew more about Denise, she didn't want Maeve getting her nose in either of their business.

Denise returned with two sandwiches and Lila's change. After hurried bites in between surges of customers, Lila showed Denise around the store and set her to shelve a new delivery of paperbacks and organizing the children's section that looked like a hurricane had just blown through. A standard day, really. There was a group of local mothers who often walked past on the way to the beach. Lila counted herself lucky that the children came through on the way to the beach, and not after. She cleaned up enough sand from the local tourists, after all. The rest of the afternoon passed quickly and Lila found time during a late afternoon lull to actually open her laptop and work briefly on her manuscript. She was finally at the part of the book where she felt the story taking shape, almost creating itself, and she felt more like a conduit than a sculptor. Which made her hope against hope that Denise might actually stay on for a while.

It would be really nice to focus on getting this manuscript done.

She looked up at the clock and realized it was already five minutes past closing. "Oh, wow. Time flies when you're having fun!" She smiled at Denise, who was working her way through organizing the romance section. "It's closing time!" She walked over to the front door and locked it, flipping the sign from open to closed.

"Are you a writer?" Denise asked, standing up and dusting her jeans off.

"I guess I am," Lila said, laughing at the puzzled expression on the woman's face. "It probably sounds silly, but I've written and self-published one book, and I'm working on a second one, and I never really thought about it until you asked." She shrugged. "I write in a vacuum. I don't talk to anyone about it because I'm writing under a pen name."

Denise smiled and raised an eyebrow suggestively. "Romance?"

"Of course." Lila answered. "Denise, I can't thank you enough for today and you starting right away."

Denise nodded, her smile fading slightly. "Sure. I mean, I was happy to help." Lila could see that Denise bit her fingernails to the quick. "Would you like for me to come back tomorrow?"

"Absolutely. Could you be here at nine? I could use you for a full nine-to-five shift if you were up to it." Lila threw up her hands. "I didn't even ask you what hours and days you're available for. And I also need to have you fill out some basic paperwork. A W-9 and all that jazz." She turned to dig under the front register. "Where are you staying, anyway? You left the home address blank."

When Denise didn't reply, Lila looked up. The woman stood there, twisting her hands, staring at her shoes.

"Denise?"

"I, uh, I've been playing it by ear. I was going to find a hotel room, but I walked in here first and well..."

Lila gaped at Denise with a mixture of shock and dismay. The town was small, with a strong tourist presence in the summer. Every beach house, cottage, and spare hotel room was likely booked already. Her new employee had nowhere to go, other than her car, for the night.

This, combined with the fear she could still see lurking beneath the surface, spurred her to action.

"Oh dear. You might have a really difficult time finding something tonight, what with all the tourists here right now."

Denise paled in response, biting her lip.

"I didn't think of that. Maybe the next town over?"

Lila shook her head. "Doubtful. The area is saturated, especially in July. Look, I have a room I sublet out of my rental house." She held up her hands at Denise's surprised stare. "I know we just met and all that. It comes furnished, and I had considered turning it into a shared room rental on Airbnb or VRBO for a little extra cash, but it's just been sitting there unoccupied. It's just for now, until you find a place of your own, or, you know, get back on your feet, but..."

"Thank you." Denise whispered, and Lila could see her fighting back tears. Her hands twisting.

"Yeah? Okay, well, my car's out front and I'm guessing that's yours down the way. I'll close up and you can just follow me to the house." Despite the tourist traffic during the day, most of the restaurants were on the opposite side of town, and the street was empty now, except for a glut of locals who were shopping at Hanniford's. Lila could see an older model Honda Civic with faded and chipped paint. Denise would never have been able to spend the night comfortably in that. Not to mention the local police were rather attentive at night. They would give her grief.

It was a short drive. Pretty much everything in Brunswick was a quick five-minute drive away, if that. As Lila pulled into the driveway of the house, and Denise parked beside her, Lila's thoughts strayed to Shane.

Mr. Pecan Pie Ellis would shit himself if he knew I had brought a practical stranger to the house. I wonder which one of his Code I'm breaking doing this?

She looked over at Denise as the young woman slung a messenger bag over her shoulder and looked like she was debating whether to get back in the car and drive far away from here.

"Come on in. I think I have some deli meat. We can make sandwiches for dinner."

Denise Fortuna was running scared. And she certainly knew what that was like. Lila was also determined to find out why. Not tonight, though. Tonight, her new employee needed food and a safe place to stay. She didn't wait for Denise to answer. She just turned on her heel and led the way to the front door.

Breaking News

Person of Interest Sought in Deadly Fire

Miami police are asking for the public's help in locating a Denise Fortuna in connection with the deadly fire on Friday that killed three young women in Little Haiti. The small home caught fire and was fully engulfed by the time Miami firefighters arrived on the scene two hours before dawn.

The fire appears intentional, according to police. One suspect, an Eddie Lamar, has a history of domestic abuse. Lamar is currently in police custody. The three victims may have already died prior to the fire.

Two of the victims were medical students at Miami Regional. As is the person of interest, Denise Fortuna, identified as a resident of the destroyed rental home.

They have identified the three victims as Taegan McMasters, Laura McCoy, and Tara Weatherby.

If you have any information on the whereabouts of Denise Fortuna, please call the Miami Police.

German Olympist Maimed in Violent Attack

Wolfgang Gestalt, a 27-year-old gold-medalist, was injured in a mugging yesterday in Bacharach, Germany. Residents of the small town are reeling at an uptick in violence in recent days. Both of Gestalt's legs were broken in the attack, and the German Olympic team manager, Friedrich Wolfson, stated that Gestalt also incurred serious head injuries. The attack occurred seconds after Gestalt stepped outside of his home yesterday evening. His attacker remains at large. He is currently in the hospital and expected to survive, but Herr Wolfson reported that the chance of Gestalt's full recovery is in question, as his legs received multiple fractures.

Gestalt has been a rising star in the German track team after rising to prominence during the last Olympics. Germany took home two Gold medals, and many speculated that Gestalt could rival Eliud Kipchoge in the men's marathon after recent sprint times beat Kipchoge's best time by nearly one minute. Now that future is in question, as the world waits to hear if Gestalt will recover.

Off to a Rough Start

The deck of cards lay before her, mocking her.

"Damn it."

Mary Shelley gazed up at her, the Boar card beside the Shelley card, an odd companion to be sure. According to the Literary Witches Oracle guidebook, the Mary Shelley card represented loss, the cycle of life, transitions and attachment. The Boar card, however, brought danger, aggression and masculinity.

"You are supposed to clarify things," she said aloud, "not make them more confusing."

A soft knock sounded at her door, and Lila jumped. It was dark, near midnight, and she had momentarily forgotten her new housemate.

"Annie?"

"Oh, hi. Come on in."

Denise pushed the door open, and it creaked loudly. She really needed to oil the hinges, and not just on this door, but all of them. Especially now that there was someone else in the house. She hadn't realized how loud the doors were, but every sound Denise made, every creak and groan, seemed to jostle her out of her focus. She had gone from writing a chapter a night to merely a few paragraphs in the past two days.

Maybe if I lay down area rugs over the wood. Perhaps that will help too.

"I was in the bathroom and heard a noise."

"Sorry, that was probably me talking to myself."

Lila looked up at Denise. She was beautiful, even with her hair a mess. Her face was pale, though, and there were still circles under her eyes. Her nails remained bitten to the quick. Despite the two of them spending not only all day at work with each other, but evenings too, Denise had remained very closed mouth about what had brought her all the way from Florida to Maine.

"I'm working on a new book and I just can't seem to figure out what's happening in it."

Denise gazed at the cards. "Are those tarot cards?"

Lila looked back at the deck in front of her. "Sort of." She pointed at a shelf to one side. It held a row of boxes. "Most of those are tarot, some oracle cards, like this deck here, and other things like the Archetypes there." She nodded at a round black box. "I use them sometimes for generating ideas or trying to figure out a direction to go." Lila touched the cards before her. "I have had little luck with Literary Witches, but I try them every so often."

"So, it tells you what to write next?" Denise asked, frowning.

Lila laughed. "No. Nothing quite like that. And often the cards just bring something random into the mix." She shrugged. "I'm not a huge believer, but every once in a while, the tarot surprises me." She frowned at the two cards. "These two, however, they just don't feel right. It's as if they match someone else, not me." Lila glanced up at Denise. "I probably sound like a loon, don't I?"

Denise stepped further into the room; her gaze fixed on the two cards. "Tell me more about these two cards."

"Um, okay, well, this card here is Mary Shelley."

"She wrote Frankenstein." Denise interrupted.

"Yeah, she did. She was just eighteen years old. Newly married to Percy Shelley. According to the guidebook, her card represents loss, the cycle of life, transitions and attachment, especially in parenthood. She bore four children, but only one survived to adulthood."

"And the other card?"

"The Boar? Well, that card represents danger, masculinity, and aggression." Lila gave a laugh. "Not anything I can use in my rom-com, to be sure." Her laugh cut short when she noticed Denise's expression. If it were possible for the girl to grow paler than she already was, Lila wasn't sure how. "Are you okay?" Denise was staring at the cards with an expression of horror. "Denise?"

"I, uh, I'd better get to bed." Denise fled through the doorway and down the hall to her bedroom. Her door shutting with a sharp click.

Lila wasn't sure what had just happened. Denise didn't strike her as conservative. Could she be uber-religious? Had Lila ended up inviting a bible-thumping ultra-conservative in her home? If so, tonight's reaction was the first sign Lila had seen of it.

Lila frowned, then stood up and stretched. Yawned. It was far too late to be fighting with her manuscript. Perhaps she could find some time tomorrow on break, or at lunch, to write more. She closed the door, turned off the lights, and stripped down to her bra and panties.

I need to buy pajamas. Can't exactly walk around the house in the nude any longer.

She closed her eyes and tried to sleep, but Denise's face, her look of horror, and the dark circles the woman still sported under her eyes continued to bother her. A mystery, really. And one she wanted to solve.

Denise had said little, but a few details had emerged over the past two days. For one, Denise had lived in Brunswick as a child, and the folks who had cared for her had owned the same bookstore Lila now ran. Denise had mentioned it the second day she worked there, as they opened it up in the morning.

She'd looked almost panicked afterward at Lila's surprised expression. "I just had fantastic memories from here. Uncle Chuck and Aunt DeeDee were so good to me. They weren't relatives, more friends of my grandparents. They raised my mom after my grandparents died in her early teens. Uncle Chuck ran the bookstore, and Aunt DeeDee had a knitting shop next door. I stayed with them for a summer, part of the fall and winter, before my mom came back and got me."

There sounded like there was a story there as well. But Denise had stopped with that, her words giving way to silence as she ran her fingers along the bookshelves, gently touching the book spines.

"Were you able to find them? Is that why you were there in the bookstore?"

Denise had shaken her head. "No, I knew they were gone. DeeDee passed away a year after I lived with them and it's been nearly twenty years. Uncle Chuck was in his late 70s when I lived here. I just, I don't know. I guess it was just the memories." She pointed to the southeast corner of the store where the non-fiction currently lived. "He had the children's section over there. A little cardboard castle with a puppet theater and beanbag chairs. I'd curl up there for hours with a pile of books. I had just learned to read the year before, and it really caught on while I was here."

After that tidbit of information, Denise had abruptly changed the subject and volunteered to work on shelving the two book orders that had come in the week before, patiently waiting in boxes in the back office.

I should just straight up ask her what is going on. I think by now, she'd trust me enough to answer with the truth.

Yesterday, near closing time, Denise had suggested they go to the grocery store and offered to buy groceries, since Lila refused to let her pay for any rent. After a disastrous attempt to make toast and eggs there at the house before they set off to work, Lila was pretty sure that Denise was catching on to what an awful cook she was. The small galley space still reeked. The toast had caught fire. And somehow, she had missed the broken eggshell in the scrambled eggs. The extra crunch was... offputting.

When Lila hesitated to name a monthly figure for rent, Denise volunteered to do the cooking. "Look, I have to do something. I can't just live here rent-free and get paid for working at the bookstore. Let me handle the meals. It will save you money on eating out, and if you don't like my cooking, I'll look up average rental prices and we can talk about numbers then. What do you say?"

Lila had happily agreed to it, and tried to pay for all the groceries. The thought of someone cooking for her was damned appealing. She hadn't had a home-cooked meal since she had called it quits with Shane and as tasty as the sandwiches from Hanniford's were, when Denise started listing off the different meals she could make, Lila was more than happy to cover the cost of the groceries. Denise, however, insisted they split the cost of the groceries and by the second evening, the refrigerator was brimming with supplies.

Denise had deftly prepared a casserole with chicken and broccoli and a layer of gooey cheese with French fried onions. "It's the ultimate comfort food. My roommates and I all loved it and took turns making it." Her smile at Lila's compliments and return for a second helping faded as she uttered the words. Before Lila could ask after them, Denise bolted for the little half bath at the base of the stairs, next to the living room that led into the postage stamp of a backyard. Above, at the top of the stairs, were the two bedrooms and a full bathroom sandwiched in between.

"Are you okay?" Lila had asked when Denise returned, her face pale.

"Yeah, my stomach's just been upset the last couple of days. Probably from traveling." She had avoided looking Lila in the eyes, one arm tucked in and around herself, as if she needed a hug. "I think I'm going to head to bed a little early. Do you need me to clean up?"

"Are you kidding? I'm eating seconds. If there's any left, I think I can handle putting it away and cleaning the dishes. Go to bed, Denise, I can handle this, no problem." As the woman turned to walk away, Lila stopped her. "Oh, and Denise? Thank you. I haven't eaten this well in, well, in six months or more. I really appreciate it."

Denise's smile had returned to her pale face. "Happy to help, Annie. It's the least I can do."

Now, hours later, Lila turned on her other side, tired, ready for sleep, except that her thoughts were busy wondering about Denise. The third day had again been unremarkable. No major revelations, but Denise seemed to be a little more relaxed. The shadows beneath her eyes were a shade lighter. She had also been highly productive. The back office was neat as a pin now, and Lila had actually written for an hour or two during the early afternoon, after Denise returned from her lunch break.

The only thing that had been of Issue was Maeve. Of course, the old busybody had blasted her way through the latest book. This wasn't particularly surprising considering that Miss Nosy Parker was desperate to impart another piece of gossip, if only to see what Lila had to say.

She had come in late in the morning, just seconds before Denise had gone on lunch break. As soon as the door chime sounded and Denise disappeared out the door and down the block, Maeve was at the counter, tapping her blood-red fingernails on the counter. Lila felt her jaw clenching in response. She forced a smile to her face. "Ready for the Shelby Von Pelt book, Maeve?"

Maeve smiled and leaned close, "In a minute. I just wondered how your new employee is doing. Denise, right? Oona, down at the thrift shop, said she was shopping for clothes in the same outfit you hired her in the other day."

"Oh really? I hadn't noticed." Lila replied, trying to unclench her teeth. She had noticed, but had said nothing. From what she could tell, Denise had two sets of scrubs and the clothes she had on her back, plus an overly large t-shirt that read "Welcome to Florida" that still had the stiff straight-off-the-hangar creases in it.

She's scared. She has no clothes, no personal effects other than what she has purchased in the past day or two. Which means she's on the run. But from what?

"And furthermore. After that? She went across the street and bought underwear, socks, a hairbrush, even a toothbrush and toothpaste at the pharmacy."

Lila struggled to hold herself back from saying something sarcastic and biting. "Okay."

Maeve looked disappointed. "Well, I just thought you should know. After all, she's staying with you, isn't she? Dolores was driving past Pineview and said she saw a battered Honda Civic with Florida plates in your driveway."

And this is when I miss city life the most. Fucking annoying is what Maeve is.

"Let me get that book for you, Maeve." She bent down and located the book set aside under the register. "Ah, here it is." She felt a surge of relief. Two more customers had queued up behind Maeve, which meant she could shoo her away. With luck, the old biddy would get the hint and make her way out the door.

Find someone else to pick on. Why don't you?

Maeve had glared at the other customers and muttered under her breath as she left, chivvied along by Lila's bright, fake smile.

As Lila turned to the other side, yet again, the time on her digital clock read 2:04. If she didn't fall asleep soon, she was going to be dead on her feet the next morning. There was another rare midsummer storm heading their way. Which meant she needed to get to the bookstore early and set out buckets upstairs. A leak had developed, and the roofers were delayed. She had a two-week wait until they could patch the roof.

What, or who, is Denise on the run from? What had her so scared?

"Tomorrow. By hook or by crook, I need to get her to talk."

Lila flipped onto her back and said, "Alexa, play meditation music." A few minutes later, her eyelashes fluttered once, twice, and she fell into a deep sleep.

Tracker

- Indalo -

The phone vibrated in the seat next to Markus as he drove. Getting a terse call from Lionel had not been the start of his day that he had expected.

Everything had gone to plan there at the small rental house in Miami. Or so he thought. Only to find out some other girl had been in his target's bed. To be honest, he hadn't known which room belonged to Denise Fortuna, so he dispatched them all. Easy enough when it looked as if they had all been drinking until past midnight. His flashlight had picked up six empty wine bottles lined up in the tiny galley kitchen. The hammer in his hand had taken care of each girl, with little or no fuss. Only one had woken as he entered the room and she had been the last. No chance to scream before he was on her, swinging the hammer down. Then it had been a simple matter of dousing the house in gas and lighting the match.

The only challenge Markus had encountered had been the urge to stay and watch the pretty flames licking the sky as the fire slid through the house, consuming everything it touched.

He'd gone to bed satisfied at a job well done. The funds had cleared the next day.

Until Alpha called. Now I'm in Dutch with the head honcho.

After a few terse words from his employer, and hours of driving later, Markus was now on the broad coastal highway heading north. He had flashed a badge at the Flying J south of Jacksonville and struck gold. Sure enough, the Fortuna girl had been here. A pimply-faced assistant manager with shaky hands had pulled up the camera footage and a few minutes later he'd seen her on the footage. Definitely not dead.

The phone vibrated again and Markus snatched it up.

"Yes?"

The girl's voice on the other end was all too familiar. He'd spoken to Lucifer a handful of times before today.

"Just got a ping off of her debit card. It looks like she used it to get some fast food about an hour ago."

"Where?"

"Zaxby's at 1372 Airport Service Road."

"Think she's heading for the airport?" Markus asked, dread forming in his gut. If she got on a plane, who knew where she would end up? He needed to catch up with her. *Now.*

"Couldn't say, but I'll let you know when it pings again."

Markus sped up on the highway. He was at least two, maybe three, days behind Fortuna and needed to catch up. He would head for the airport.

An hour later, Markus pressed the buttons on his phone, snarling with frustration. A click and the girl's voice sounded bored.

"Lucifer speaking."

"You sent me to a fucking pet airport?" He hissed.

"I did no such thing. I gave you the address for Zaxby's, the site of the last debit card ping." Lucifer answered. "What you did with that information is not my problem."

His hand strayed to the handle of the hammer. The claw end, cleaned of every speck of hair and blood, was nestled deep within the car seat cushions. He fought to contain his rage. How he would love to sink it deep into the girl's head like he had the three young women at the rental house. He bit his tongue.

"I need more information."

"When I have it, I'll call you. She will need to stop at some point." Lucifer's voice was calm, indifferent. "Now, unless you needed something else..." The phone beeped as Markus slammed a finger down on the disconnect button.

The next ten days unspooled slowly. And for Markus, who prided himself on his quick turnaround times for targets, it was maddening. He didn't spend days following a target. He got in, got the job done, and back out. Lucifer's brief text informed him that Fortuna had withdrawn a significant amount of cash from an ATM on the second day, which wasn't surprising given that her face was plastered on news bulletins throughout Florida. But he figured she would have to come up for air soon.

When the next ping rolled in, it was a gas station in New York, and Markus felt a rush of pain as a tension headache rolled in. His target had made it to New York three days ago, on a Friday. Thanks to delays in bank reporting, Lucifer hadn't seen it come in until the close of Monday. Markus headed north. The next employee he saw was not as easy to impress with a badge.

"I think you gotta have a warrant or something before we hand over anything to the police. And that ain't a New York badge." The thin, greasy-haired man with acne and an odd facial tic said, then shuffled away from the bulletproof glass. Markus had tried threats, but the attendant looked unimpressed and returned to watching some wrestling match on his cracked cell phone, ignoring Markus until he left.

The rain and the wind from the approaching storm had driven him back inside of his car where he had glared through the rain pelting the windshield and cursed the attendant. Markus contemplated waiting until the man's shift ended, and then killing him, but the streets were busy and potential witnesses numbered in the dozens even now, in late evening. He didn't have time for this. He needed to find the girl and finish her. Markus didn't know what she had done to piss off Alpha, and he didn't particularly care. It wasn't in his job description.

A police car moved down the street slowly. He ignored it and contemplated what to do. If she was here, in New York, it would be even harder for him to track her. The city was vast. He picked up his phone and dialed Lucifer. He could hear the sounds of a battle in the background.

"Lucifer here."

"Does Fortuna have any connections in New York? Any friends? Anyone she would go to?"

Lucifer muted the sounds of the battle with a sharp click and he could hear additional rapid mouse clicks as she accessed the vast amount of illicit info at her fingertips. A few seconds of silence later, and she answered.

"I've got nothing. She's lived all over the U.S., but never in New York, only..."

"Only what?"

"Hold on." More clicks and rapid typing followed. "Brunswick, Maine."

"What's in Maine?"

"Probably nothing, but she lived there for around a year as a kid. I'm seeing school records from a Kate Furbish Elementary School. The only place on the east coast besides Florida that she's been. Other than that, it was flyover country and Georgia, Alabama, the Dakotas. I'm not saying she is in Maine," He could practically hear her shrug, "but that would be my guess at where to try next."

"Maine is over three hundred miles away."

Lucifer sounded bored. "Yeah? So?"

He hung up the phone.

Someday, she'll fuck up. And when she does, I hope they send me to take care of the uppity bitch.

He loved his job. There was something very special about taking a life - human or otherwise. To watch as the light in the eyes faded, and death erased everything a creature was from the world. Given his druthers, he preferred to take his time. What greater pleasure was there than seeing another person's pain?

His first try at ending the target had been rushed. The girls were in multiple rooms, so it had to be quick. He hadn't known which room was hers and time had been of the essence. He hadn't wanted her or the others she shared the house with sounding the alarm. It had left him feeling unfulfilled, dissatisfied. Worse, learning that he had missed the target had been humiliating. That had never happened before, and he was still smarting over it. He would make it better, however. When he found her, and he would, he would kill the girl slowly and savor every minute. Maybe he would keep a piece of her as a trophy.

For now, however, he had a decision to make. He sat there, the phone in his hand, and noticed the same police car drive by again. Slower this time. Had the attendant said something? Called someone? As soon as it eased past, around the corner, he started the car up, and cut in front of a truck, turned left at the next intersection, and entered Brunswick, Maine, into his GPS. He checked his watch. If he drove straight through, he would arrive before dawn. And if Lucifer steered him wrong, and the girl wasn't there, maybe he could lay the groundwork to have Lucifer replaced with someone far more capable.

The rain fell steadily as he made his way out of the Big Apple on the FDR and headed north again, along I-95. A massive wreck slowed his progress considerably. By the time he entered Connecticut, the rain had stopped. The clouds above hung low, blotting out the stars in this unsettled open land, which was a rarity on the over-populated East coast. A storm was brewing in the Atlantic, one threatening to become far more dangerous and violent. Markus drove on, the car eating the miles steadily. By three, however, he was feeling the missing hours of sleep far more than he preferred.

He pulled off the road when he saw the sign for a Rodeway Inn in Tolland. He'd get a night's rest, then move on in the morning. Maybe leave early, by five, before the sun rose. Markus set a ball cap on his head and headed into the motel office. A pimple-faced kid took his money and handed him a key without a word. The boy didn't look at his face or compare it with the driver's license, which Markus preferred. The likeness was close enough, but the previous owner of the license had died, rather suddenly, soon after obtaining the renewal. As far as the world at large was concerned, Andrew Talbot had simply disappeared, leaving his elderly mother and two ex-wives behind one fine summer's day two years ago. It would be another four years before Markus needed to worry about a finding someone else who looked like him, and hopefully one who had fewer family ties than dear Andrew had. It was easier that way.

Markus had conveniently parked near his room. And it was easier to leave the car where it was and avoid most of the downpour by staying underneath the overhang and following it to his room. The room was a standard no frills kind of place. As Markus tossed his damp backpack on the floor near the desk, his burner phone rang. It wasn't *his* number. Which meant it was likely *Beta*.

Shit.

He pressed the button and put the phone to his ear. "Yes?"

"What's your status?"

"I'm a four-hour drive from Brunswick, Maine."

"You aren't on the road." A statement, not a question.

"I needed to stop. It was slow going because of the storm. I will be there by morning."

Beta did not sound happy. "See that you are. I want this girl removed from play immediately."

"Yes, ma'am."

The phone beeped in response as she disconnected. Markus tossed it onto the bed, then stared at it, concern swirling. It was one thing for Alpha to be involved, and another for Beta to step forward. It meant he was well and truly fucked if he didn't get ahold of the girl and finish the job, once and for all.

Sleep, as much as he needed it, eluded him. Markus tossed and turned. The howl of the wind outside felt in tune with his own unease. He dreamed intermittently, his fingers unconsciously seeking the symbol inked in red on his wrist. Markus woke long before dawn and gave up on sleeping in disgust. He'd sleep when the mark was dead.

By the time he arrived in Brunswick, the sun had risen into the sky, but Markus couldn't see it. The dark clouds on the horizon warned of the impending storm. He'd heard all about it, the constant, repetitive stream of news as he drove, rain and wind lashing the world outside. Finally, tiring of the endless comparisons to Hurricane Carol that apparently had hit the region back in the 50s, he switched stations until he hit a classical station unperturbed by the storm heading their way. Through the downpour, he glanced around for a coffee shop and his eyes fell on a sign... Hanniford's. It didn't look like a cafe, more of a small grocer. He would stop there, get a sandwich and find out where he could find a coffee.

Street parking meant that it soaked him the second he stepped out of his car. The temperature had risen to a balmy 80 degrees, and the water falling from the sky felt warm instead of cold.

As if the sky were taking a great piss.

He hurried inside of the quaint grocery store and strode toward the delicatessen. Moments later, sandwich in hand, Markus waited at the register. Behind him stood a curious busybody who seemed to examine every inch of him.

If she doesn't stop staring at me, I'll throttle the old cow.

A young woman jogged up to the cash register, wiping her hands on a towel before shoving one end in her jeans. "Sorry to keep you waiting!" She rang Markus up. "That will be $7.25, sir." As she handed Markus his change, she smiled at the woman behind him. "Good morning, Maeve. How are you?"

There was a small alcove near the doors. Markus could see it held two small tables and chairs. He settled into one, his eyes focused on the food, ignoring the women. He would eat this and then see if he couldn't find the girl, make inquiries.

"Good morning, Andie. I came into town to get a new book, but the store isn't open yet. So I figured I would come and pick up a few things." The woman sniffed, glanced his way, and then away again. "Can you believe she hired that girl, the new one in town? Without so much as a by your leave, or asking if anyone could recommend anyone."

Andie said nothing. She just shrugged and rang up the older woman's groceries. "That'll be $24.18."

Maeve reached into her wallet and handed the younger woman a card. "I mean, I know Angela was just as flaky as could be, but I've known her since she was in diapers. Now another new girl breezes in, a complete stranger, and that Brewer gal immediately hires her. I can't say I care much about the way this town is changing. It's being invaded by outsiders."

"Oh Maeve, Denise is really nice. Just the other day, she saw Dale shoplifting and said something in time for Uncle Lyle to stop him. And it was a high-ticket item."

Markus' ears perked up. *Denise. From out of town? That couldn't be a coincidence.*

"Well, perhaps if she were focusing on her job, the bookstore would be open by now." Maeve snapped back, a disgruntled tone in her voice.

The girl sighed. "Have a good day, Maeve."

The older woman shook her head in disgust, glared at Markus as she walked past, and retrieved an umbrella from the floor next to the door. Another disgruntled "Hmph!" and she stepped outside, disappearing into the deluge. He watched as she marched across the street and down to the end, huddled under her umbrella for a long moment as she peered into the bookstore window, then straightened and walked off. The bookstore was dark, the front parking empty now that Maeve had gotten into her car and driven off.

A little B and E, a look through the office records, and I see what I can find.

He finished his sandwich, brushed the crumbs from his hands, tossed the remnants of the sandwich into the trash before he headed out, turning right instead of left. He would circle the block, see if there was a back door, and then apply one of the few non-violent skills he had learned in his teen years, lock-picking, to gain entry. It was one talent that had brought him to the attention of the Indalo two decades ago. If his target had made her way to Brunswick and was now working in a bookstore, he would soon find out. And following that, well, he would do what he did best.

It Wasn't Me

- Lila -

For an instant, between the gloom in her normally bright bedroom and a fading dream of Shane's slow, sensuous kisses, Lila was confused by the sound she was hearing. It was morning, although the sky outside was overcast and dark. Lila was shocked she had overslept. It wasn't as if it mattered that much. It was Sunday, after all. And she opened the store at noon on Sundays, even in summer. But normally she was awake at sunrise, or even earlier, now that it was warm out. The storm had changed that, apparently.

There was something about warm weather, spring and summer, that put a lightness in her step and energized her. Fall and winter always felt like death and spread over the land. A time to burrow deep and sleep. She wrote more in the summer. Which seemed ridiculous, really. She had bemoaned her situation to Margery once.

"There's nothing to do in the winter. It's the perfect time for writing. But am I writing? No! I just want to sleep all day and drink hot chocolate!"

The sound came again. This time, Lila was awake enough to recognize it. It was indisputably the sound of retching. It seemed her new roommate was unwell.

She slipped out of bed, reached for her deodorant and dressed. As Lila emerged from her room, Denise was exiting the bathroom, her skin pale, with the circles under her eyes even more pronounced.

"A touch of the stomach flu? Or my cooking?" She asked the young woman, fearing it might have been the latter, more than she was concerned about Denise spreading the flu to her. She was rarely ill.

Denise opened her mouth to answer, then just as quickly shut it. Her eyes panicked as she spun on her heel. She ran back inside the bathroom, and the door slammed behind her. More retching sounds.

"Yikes." Lila stared at the closed door for a moment and then headed downstairs. She would use the half bath down there and then fix some cereal. The last thing that her roommate needed was the smell of something cooking in the air.

Especially my cooking. I'll burn it to hell and back, anyway.

A few minutes later, sitting in the tiny kitchen, she flipped on the tv in the living room to the news. The weather would be on soon and she wanted to check on Hurricane Agnes, which had turned from a tropical storm into a far more serious hurricane yesterday. Hurricanes this far up the eastern seaboard were rare, but even this far north, they could actually be a problem. Lila had never been in a hurricane. The thought of it was rather exhilarating, honestly, although she was more worried about how to prepare for one. Did she need to put boards up on the windows? Would she need to leave if it headed towards them? Maeve had, of course, told her all about some family with beachfront property who stayed instead of leaving when they were warned to.

"Those poor children watched their father washed away in the floodwaters." Maeve had said the day before, crocodile tears glittering in her eyes. "Although, I'm not one to gossip, but their mother remarried less than a year later. To the husband's best friend, no less. It makes one wonder, it really does."

Lila shook her head. Maeve was a piece of work, she really was. She pointed the remote at the television, turned up the volume, and spooned cereal into her mouth.

"And next up we have our meteorologist, Anthony Parker, to weigh in on the prospects for some rather severe weather by the end of the week." A peppy blond in a sleek red dress chirped. "Anthony? What's the scoop on Hurricane Agnes?"

"Thanks Tiffany. Well, it looks like Agnes is continuing to gather in strength. She is now registering as a Category Two, with 97 mile per hour winds recorded this morning by the NOAA. And she is continuing to make her way north along the eastern coastline. Now, as you may already know, a Category Two storm can cause storm surges of six to eight feet, and endanger those in mobile homes, damage roofs, and cause flooding."

Denise appeared at the foot of the stairs. She walked into the kitchen, looking pale and wretched.

"So sorry."

Lila swallowed her mouthful. "Don't be. Hopefully, you will feel better now. I don't know about you, but once I throw up, I always feel better after." She pointed at her cereal. "Do you... want any?"

Denise shook her head and grimaced. "No, I think I'll just stick to water." She pulled a cup from the drain tray and filled it at the tap.

"Back to you, Tiffany." The meteorologist grinned, and the camera panned back to the blond bombshell in red.

"Thanks Anthony. Police are asking for help as the search continues for a person of interest in the mysterious fire and deaths of three young women in Miami, Florida, nearly two weeks ago. Miami police are asking for anyone who knows of the whereabouts of Denise Fortuna, age 25, a nursing student at Miami Regional and recently employee of Happy Haven Retirement Village, to please contact local authorities. The police do not consider Fortuna a suspect. Instead, they are concerned for her safety after a deadly fire broke out at the home she shared with two other roommates. Both roommates and a friend of Ms. Fortuna were in the house. Ms. Fortuna has not been seen since. The Miami County medical examiner's office released the autopsy reports on the three victims, showing they died of blunt force trauma *before* the flames broke out. Fire investigators declared it a crime scene after evidence of an accelerant was used, but police say the victims were already dead."

Lila sat, spoon in hand, gaping at the television in shock as they showed a photo of Denise, likely her student photo since she was wearing scrubs, on the television screen, before turning her gaze toward her new roommate.

The glass in Denise's hand fell with a crash to the ground. Glass splintering. If Lila had thought the girl looked pale before, it was nothing compared to now.

"Denise? What is going on?"

"I didn't hurt my friends. It wasn't me. They..." Whatever she had intended to say next was lost as she threw up violently all over the kitchen floor.

Suddenly, and not unsurprisingly, Lila's appetite vanished. She stood up, glanced at the television where the anchor was describing Denise's car and license plate. Then a litter of rolling, rollicking puppies took over the screen. She looked at Denise, who was holding onto the countertop, white-knuckles gripping the edge, still heaving.

"I'm... I'm sorry." She whispered, tears gathering in her eyes.

"Don't be," Lila said, letting the paper towels sop up the mess. She passed Denise a couple of them, and Denise wiped her mouth and then burst into tears. Lila skirted the mess and walked over to her, put her arm around her, and guided Denise to the table.

"Okay. Sit down. Just sit down and breathe, okay?"

A moment later, she had a box of Kleenex in hand, and another glass of water, along with a half pack of saltines. The saltines were likely stale, but Lila knew they would be the most that Denise could stomach, and from the way she was swaying, she needed something more than water in her stomach.

Denise sobbed for several minutes. Tears rolled down her cheeks. She gasped for breath, and her slight frame shook.

"I need... I need..."

Lila reached across the table. If Denise was putting on a show, it was one hell of one, and from Lila's perspective, she was for real, or one hell of an actress. She patted Denise's hand.

"Take your time. Just... breathe... okay?"

The younger woman nodded and burst into a fresh round of tears that lasted for several minutes. Lila hadn't known Denise long, but she seemed gentle. Lila couldn't imagine for an instant that it was Denise who had killed her roommates. That she had run, though, completely *left* the area. Now that was odd.

Lila remembered when the incident had occurred, just a day or two before Denise had walked into the bookstore. They had thought it was the three roommates, Lila was sure she remembered that much. But now it was apparently two of the roommates and a friend who didn't live there. At the first mention of it in the news, they had pointed the finger at a local man. Was he still a suspect? There was so much she didn't know.

No matter what, if I know now, so does Maeve. The old biddy lives and dies by the morning news. Which means we have hours, at most, before someone will be at our door.

Denise was calming. The sobs slowing. She wiped her eyes, blew her nose, and sipped the water. She let out a slow, shuddering sigh.

"I'm sorry."

Lila chose her words carefully. "Denise, you don't need to be sorry. But I think you need someone to talk to. If not me, then..."

"You. I know I can trust you. I mean, you took me in without question." Denise said, interrupting her. "I have told no one. I've been too scared. He's powerful. Rich."

Denise sucked in a breath and spoke then. The story spilled out of her in a flood, combined with more tears, and Lila sat there stunned, mouth hanging open. The silence hung between them.

"You don't believe me," Denise said softly, miserably. "And if you don't believe me, what good will going to the police do? It's hearsay."

Lila reached out and took the girl's hand. "I believe you, Denise. I do. Because I've been in a situation of my own. It wasn't exactly like yours, but still." She squeezed Denise's hand and then released it, frowning. "What concerns me is that everyone is seeing this broadcast. This is a small town and news spreads fast, especially with people like Maeve."

"I'm so..."

"Don't say it." Lila held up a warning finger. "Just don't."

She dug into her back pocket, pulled out her phone, and stared at it.

"What are you going to do?" Denise asked, her voice rising, her fear apparent.

"I'm going to get us help." Lila answered, frowning.

"Wait, I..." Denise rose, shakily, "I should just go. If I go now..."

"If you run, you look like you have something to hide," Lila said, looking up.

"The police will never believe me. I have no proof! And he's rich, powerful."

"I know. I'm not talking about going to the police. Look, I know someone who can help. Someone who can get you somewhere safe."

Denise stared at her. "What does that even mean? Nowhere is safe! They think I had something to do with it. A person of interest. That's as good as them saying I killed my friends. My *best* friends. I can't..." She sunk back down in her chair, hid her face in her hands.

"I need to make a call, Denise. But I promise you, I can help you. *He* can help you. I'd bet my life on it."

Denise stared at her with red-rimmed, puffy eyes. She dragged a Kleenex across her nose and sucked in a shuddering breath.

"Who?"

Lila grimaced. "The last person I want to call. Believe me." She typed in his number and listened as the phone rang three times before he answered.

The Last Person I Expected to Call

-Shane-

On the flight out, Shane had convinced himself that Luke was pulling his leg. Surely Tapeesa, who had buried her husband some eight or nine years earlier, wasn't setting her sights on him. He'd been visiting Luke's cabin in Alaska at least twice a year for the past three years. And with it, had come regular visits to Tapeesa's sprawling, ramshackle property. As Luke's nearest neighbor, and just a half mile down the road, Tapeesa and her family ran a 500-acre section that included a herd of yak, reindeer, goats and chickens. She was a short, stout Inuit woman. There were more kids on the property than were hers. Shane wasn't sure where they all came from, but you couldn't swing a stick and not hit one of them. They ran about, helping with the farm, playing games, drawing, and building. The last time he visited, there were at least two small houses and a boat, all in various stages of completion. Between chickens running loose, a half dozen cats and dogs, and the ever-wily escapee goat, it was absolute chaos there. The kids would follow Luke and Shane around like lemmings, eager to help, full of questions. And although Tapeesa always seemed to need some kind of help, Shane had enjoyed visiting. It was a world vastly different from the one he had grown up in with just his mother and no siblings.

He decided he would skip the yak slaughtering. Hell, maybe he would even put his feet up in the hammock that Luke had installed out back and relax, read a book.

Shane's plans, however, hadn't included one very pissed off skunk and a curious young bear. Nor had they included having to wash the bear cub inside the cabin in the bathtub, which meant the smell of skunk permeated every inch of the cabin the next day as Sue whined in the corner of his cage and sneezed repeatedly.

Damnitall, I've probably given him a cold.

It had turned out that Sue was a boy, not a girl. This had come as a surprise to Shane. Then again, trust Luke to not mention that minor fact. Shane had found a recipe for removing skunk smell on dogs online and figured it would work just as well for the bear cub. A mixture of dish soap with hydrogen peroxide and baking soda had done the trick, but Sue had squealed and fought the bath valiantly, splashing Shane until the front of his clothes were soaked through.

After he locked Sue into the wire kennel inside of the cabin where Pepe would be less offended by the bear cub's presence, Shane wrung out his clothes as best he could and ran them out on the clothesline to dry. Pepe, Luke's three-legged skunk, sniffed the drips and looked at Shane with curiosity. The cat food that Sue had scattered widely in his frenzy to escape the skunk spray had been devoured, and it seemed Pepe was hoping for more.

"Fine. Fine. I'll give you a little more." Shane grumbled, his eyes watering as he stood mere feet from the pungent creature.

"You know that talking to animals is the first sign of insanity." Shane turned to see Tapeesa's oldest, Hanta, standing a few feet away, a package tucked under his arm.

"And here I thought the Inuit talked to the animals." Shane countered.

The younger man snorted. "Ah, yes, Inuit talk big wampum to spirit animal." He rolled his eyes at Shane. "My mother sent me over with some reindeer sausage for your breakfast. She says to show up by noon."

So much for lazing out on the hammock with a book.

"Should I bring anything?" Shane asked, taking the package from Hanta. It was warm to the touch. The accompanying aroma of sausage and spices woke his stomach, despite the odoriferous presence of the skunk by his feet. Pepe ignored him, eating his cat food, stopping only to look toward the cabin door. Inside, Sue wailed his distress at being confined to the dog kennel.

"Nah, we got everything we need. See you there." He turned and left, disappearing into the forest.

Shane unwrapped the sausage, pulling off a chunk for the skunk at his feet. He tossed it a few feet out in the yard and Pepe looked up at him briefly, then did his funny three-legged hop walk out to where it had landed and chowed down.

"I better take the rest inside before you insist on more." Shane said. He walked inside and instantly Sue was on his back legs, his black button nose sniffing the air. "Well, shit, forgot about you." He slid a chunk through the metal bars and Sue pounced on it as if he were starving and hadn't eaten in days instead of a mere hour between eating his own food and attempting to take Pepe's.

"And we all know how that went, don't we?" Shane said to the cub, as the tiny cub devoured the chunk of meat. Sue had to weigh all of ten pounds at most. A mere fraction of the 400 pound behemoth he would grow up to be. As he was now, the wire kennel that Luke had wouldn't last longer than a month, possibly two, before the creature became large enough and strong enough to bend the wires. Luke would be back long before then, three weeks at the most.

The cub had practically inhaled the chunk he had given him. Shane looked at the package. Tapeesa had sent over six sausages, and between Pepe and Sue, he was now down to five. Shane reached for the fresh eggs that sat on the counter, cracked five of them into a skillet, and scrambled them. A few minutes later, he sat at the tiny dining table and divided the eggs and three sausage links between his plate and Sue's never-ending stomach. He had two sausages left to eat for breakfast to-morrow, or a snack tonight if he was feeling peckish.

Slight chance of that. Tapeesa's fry bread and the fresh yak-a-dillas will fill me to bursting.

He checked the time. There was enough for a brief nap on the hammock if he wanted, but when he stood to walk out, there was Pepe, on the hammock, belly full, making himself comfortable.

"I don't know how you do it, man, but damned if I'm going to spoon with a skunk." Shane said aloud, shaking his head. Pepe was friendly enough, but the smell was overwhelming. Caught in a trap, his front left leg had been too badly damaged by the time Luke had found him. He'd freed Pepe, nursed him back from the brink of death, and the creature had kept him company ever since. Shane had asked Luke once why he hadn't had the creature's glands removed, since he was more of a pet now than wild.

Luke had shrugged and said, "He was born wild. He should stay that way. The scent glands are his defense. I can't take away his freedom to run about, and if I did, it would change him in ways that the missing leg never could."

Still, it was a little more up close and personal than Shane felt like getting with Pepe. He leaned back on the bed, kicked off his shoes, and reached for a book. Despite the small size of the cabin, one that Luke had built himself, there was an entire wall dedicated to books. Luke was an omnivorous reader. He had everything from non-fiction to dystopi-an, history to sci-fi, and more. It seemed he had even organized them into separate genres. His gaze fell on the sci-fi section. He could see Asi-mov, Clarke, Herbert, Hogan, and more. One book caught his eye. A planet and spaceship on the front cover. "G581: The Departure. Huh." It looked well worn. As if Luke had read it more than once. He settled back and read, stopping only when Sue pawed at the cage door an hour later, obviously wanting to go outside. By then, Pepe had disappeared from the hammock, and from view, no doubt deep in the woods by now. He released Sue and watched the baby bear bound away toward the tree line and disappear. The cub would be back. He never went far, according to Luke, and it was nearly time to leave. A walk through the woods to Tapeesa's place would allow him to stretch his legs. The weather was excellent for it.

He could hear the kids long before he could see them. If it hadn't had been for their higher voices and the occasional shriek of laughter, he would have thought there was a war ahead. Instead, as he threaded his way through a large thicket of trees, which opened onto the western edge of Tapeesa's property, he could see some kind of water balloon fight going on. At least, it had started out as a water balloon fight, if the dots of color that littered the ground were any sign. Every kid was soaked to the bone. A handful had armed themselves with buckets of water, a couple of others were tussling over the garden hose, and he could see Kaya, Tonraq, and Meriwa still held several balloons each and were holding their own. Not bad for being the youngest and smallest of Tapeesa's offspring. Unlike their rather swarthy older brothers and sisters, the triplets were small-boned, almost willowy. It was such a stark difference from their elder siblings that if Shane were to guess; he was sure they were half-siblings to the rest. There were at least a half-dozen additional kids running about, possibly more, most of them screaming in a blend of Tlingit and English.

His arrival did not go unnoticed, however, and some kids had rather feral grins on their faces. Shane threw up his hands. "I'm a neutral party to this conflict! I'm Switzerland! You want help with some yak-killing. You best leave me out of your war!"

Hanta yelled in Tlingit and the handful of kids heading his way with chaos in their eyes slowed and turned away. Shane saluted him and headed for the barn where a small group of men and women had gathered. Tapeesa grinned at him broadly, then called out to the screaming children. Silence fell.

"Damn kids gonna scare the yaks with all that screaming. Make their meat taste off." She grumbled under her breath, then reached for his arm, pulled him down to her level and planted a smacking kiss on his forehead. "Good to see you, Ellis."

"Same. Thanks for the tasty reindeer sausage."

"Wait until you taste the yak-a-dillas. They taste better when the meat's fresh." She winked at him, handed him a sharp knife, said something in Tlingit to an older man a few feet away, then nudged Shane to join the group.

It had rather surprised Shane to find that yaks, unlike cattle, had little or no smell. They also didn't moo as much as they grunted. Despite the grunts, they still reminded him of hairy cows. He was relieved when the others took the lead, leading one yak far from the small group they had penned into the corral and handled the slaughter quickly and efficiently. After the beast was dead, they raised it up on hooks, drained the carcass, and got to work. Shane was pretty sure that after this, he would never eat meat again.

By the time he and the others finished dressing the five yaks, nearly five hours later, his empty stomach insisted that he absolutely could, and should, try one of the yak-a-dillas he had heard so much about. His muscles ached from helping to heave each thousand pound carcass into the air and then carefully remove the hide with a sharp knife. His clothes were bloody and caked in mud from one particularly energetic bull who was not going out without a fight. And despite looking as if he had played a grotesque part in a horror film, Shane sank down at the picnic table and dug into the yak-a-dillas stacked on his plate with gusto. They weren't strikingly different from shredded beef, and Tapeesa made a mean Pico de gallo to go with it. The other adults sunk into seats near him. The constant chatter in a Tlingit faded away as the adults tucked away stacks of the yak-a-dillas, Pico de gallo, and a pile of fry bread.

The sun was still high in the sky at seven, as Shane headed back to the cabin.

Tomorrow, I'm damned well sleeping in. I don't care what they want done, I'm saying "no."

They filled the sack in his hand with yak-a-dillas. A large grocery sack of them. Enough to slip plenty of the foil-wrapped delights into the freezer for Luke to chow down on.

He was tired, worn out from the hacking and slicing he had done. The only thing on his mind was Luke's Japanese-style soaking tub and a good night's rest. Sue met him along the way, giving a squeaky half-purr, half-rumble, as Shane tossed the beast two of the yak-a-dillas and closed the bear into his kennel.

An hour later, his eyes closed and his breathing slowing, the sound of his ringer ripped Shane from his sleep. "Christ, what now?" He reached for a towel, stepped out of the tub, and caught the phone before it went to voicemail.

"Ellis."

"Shane? It's Lila."

He could hear it in her voice. She sounded worried, maybe even afraid. "Lila? What's wrong?"

He listened as she explained the predicament. He asked a couple of questions. It was clear Lila's friend needed help.

"You were right to call. Head to the address I'm texting to you now. It should take you around four hours, maybe a little more, to get there." The phone chimed at the other end. "Take both cars, but switch the girl's plates with the set I left you in case of emergencies, and have her park it in the satellite airport parking. That'll slow things down, make you harder to track. Drive 1-2 miles over the speed limit. This attracts less attention than driving the speed limit or below. Don't stop for gas or anything else until you are well out of town. Park your car inside of the garage of the safe house. Stay put inside. The kitchen has basic supplies, and I'll be there by late afternoon with some more."

"Okay. Got it." Lila paused. "And Shane? Thank you."

Shane could hear another voice in the background ask, "Who *is* that?"

And in the half-second before Lila disconnected the call, he heard her reply, "The last person I ever expected to talk to again."

He stood there, staring at the phone in his hand. The call ended, the screen black. She didn't call him because she wanted him back. She called him because of what he did. The very thing that had driven them apart was forcing them together again.

"*You* were the last person I expected to call," Shane said in return, his words unheard by anyone save himself and a bear cub gently snoring in his kennel.

He scheduled the red-eye flight and checked the time. He had enough time to drive to the ferry and the airport with an hour or two to spare. As he drove, his thoughts circled from Lila's face to her body nestled against his.

She needs your help, that's all. Keep it professional, Ellis. Keep your dick in your pants.

The sun held its own near the horizon. By the time the plane took off, he could expect around a brief twilight that would darken only as the plane moved further south and then back to sunlight as he headed east.

Hours later, the traveling, his work dressing the yak meat, and more, caught up to him. He relaxed, leaned his seat back, and closed his eyes. Lila was waiting for him, and she needed his help. When he got to her, he'd keep it professional, like he should have done to begin with.

My Name is Lila

- Lila -

"I can't believe this is happening." Denise said. Lila had lost count of how many times her new friend had said it in the past hour.

Then again, Lila hadn't been sure that Denise wouldn't rabbit on her during the drive to the airport. She had followed Denise's car closely. The new plates she had dug out of the closet were from North Dakota and would definitely throw off anyone looking for them. Denise hadn't rabbited, which was good, and now they were well on their way to the address Shane texted her. It was a long drive, another two hours or more before they arrived, but Lila was confident they had left in time and there wasn't anyone following them.

Shane said he will be there this evening.

The thought of seeing him again, for the first time in six months, made her stomach give a nervous twist. Which then morphed into a memory of his hands on her and a wave of desire rushed through her.

No, no, no! You are not getting back in bed with that man, no matter how sexy he is!

"Annie?" Denise's voice brought Lila back to the present. "What's wrong?"

"Hm?"

"You were glaring just now. You just looked so, I don't know, so *angry*. I've gotten you involved in my mess. This is all my fault."

Lila spared a quick glance away from the road as Denise buried her face in her hands.

"Hey, come on now. You have done nothing wrong, Denise. Nothing at all. And I'm not mad at you, really, I'm not. I was just remembering something, that's all."

A few moments of silence passed before Denise sat up and asked.

"Is it Shane?"

"What?"

"Whoever had you looking like you wanted to punch someone in the throat? I figured it had to be this Shane guy because of the way you talked to him on the phone."

Lila gave a rueful laugh. "Yeah, Shane has a lot to do with why I was glaring. We dated for a while. It didn't work out. And I guess it's still a bit of a sore spot for me."

"And this is the guy we are meeting?"

Lila sighed. "Yeah."

"There's a story here, isn't there?"

"Yeah, there is. And it starts with me telling you that my name isn't Annie Brewer."

She snuck a look at Denise's face. The younger woman's eyes, still red-rimmed from crying, had widened.

"It's... not?"

A sign for Burger King appeared along the road and Lila's stomach growled for something, anything, past the cereal she had eaten hours ago.

"How do you feel about getting some fast food?" Lila asked, abruptly changing the subject. "My treat."

"Okay."

Silence returned for the two miles it took before the exit appeared. Lila turned off of the highway and made a left, following the signs for the Burger King.

"I'm just going to go through the drive-thru, okay?"

Denise nodded wordlessly.

They ordered two combo meals and Denise handed Lila her food, her own fingers picking at her fries, nibbling at one before shoving it *back in the* bag. Lila parked the car in the crowded parking lot and tore into her burger. The air felt heavy between them - full of questions. She had downed her third bite of a burger before Denise set her food down, turned toward her.

"I can't stand it anymore. Who are you? What's your real name? Are you on the run too?"

Lila sighed, finished chewing, and set the burger down.

"My name is Lila Benoit. I've been in WitSec, witness protection, for just over two and a half years now. And at the rate the FBI's investigation is going, I might never go back to my old life. In fact, I'd say it's highly unlikely."

Denise stared at her, eyes round. She swallowed convulsively. "And people in Witness Protection are supposed to keep a low profile, aren't they?"

Lila laughed, "Yeah, well..."

Denise buried her face in her hands. "I've brought this down on you. I'm so sorr..."

"Don't do that. Don't apologize. I knew the minute you walked into the bookstore that you needed help." Lila sighed, "I guess I just never expected things to go quite like this. I can't tell you much of why I'm in WitSec. Honestly, you have enough on your plate already. All I can say is that I saw something I shouldn't, and until they can find out who the puppeteers are, the real bad guys, then I'll have to stay in hiding."

They sat in silence for a while longer, finishing their food before Lila started the car and pulled back onto the highway. The sun was still high in the sky, but Lila glanced at the clock, feeling a sudden urgency.

"We need to hurry. I want to get there before dark."

Denise nodded and Lila pressed her foot down on the gas, driving faster now, feeling conflicted, and yet somehow eager to see Shane again. As they got closer to their destination, Lila could feel her nerves ramping up. She hadn't seen Shane in six months, not since he had broken her heart and left her alone and vulnerable. Despite this, she couldn't help but remember the way her body responded to him, the memory of his fingers trailing down her spine, and the way his body felt against hers. After two hours of driving, they pulled off the highway and onto a quiet rural road.

The address Shane had texted them led them to a secluded two-story cabin in the woods, surrounded by robust maple trees and the faint scent of jasmine in the air. The cabin looked new, the surrounding ground disturbed, rough, all indicative of new construction.

Lila parked the car in front of the garage and glanced at Denise.

"This is it," Lila said.

"Is anyone here?" Denise asked as they stepped out of the car. The sun was lowering in the sky, with plenty of light left, but the property looked empty.

"He mentioned getting here after sunset, so no, but there's a door code in the text he sent. Hold on." Lila thumbed through her phone until she found what she was looking for, typed the code in and heard the door lock click.

She turned the handle and opened the door to the cabin.

The interior was dimly lit, and the air smelled of cedar and fresh paint. Lila stepped inside and looked around. It had a rustic charm to it, with a spacious living room complete with a fireplace, a cozy-looking kitchen, and a steep wooden staircase leading up to the second floor, likely where the bedrooms were. The living room sported hardwood floors with wide, honey-colored planks and heavy wood beams ran across the ceiling. A mantel over the fireplace was pristine. The fireplace clearly had never been used. There was a marble island, and black granite countertops. The kitchen was equally spotless, with pots and pans hanging from the pot rack over the kitchen island, waiting to be used. Their footsteps echoed on the hardwood floors, and the sun streamed in through the windows, the room illuminated in a warm glow. A soft breeze rustled the leaves outside, and from far off, she could hear the birds chirping. Denise followed her inside, looking around nervously.

"Do you think he'll be here soon?" Denise asked, her voice barely above a whisper.

Lila shrugged, "I don't know. He didn't say. But I need to move the car into the garage and figure out the room situation upstairs."

After Lila drove the car into the adjoining garage, and they had brought their meager belongings into the house, the two women explored the rest of the house.

As they made their way up the stairs, Lila's thoughts strayed to Shane's imminent arrival. She couldn't help but feel her heart beat faster with anticipation. She hadn't seen Shane in so long, and she wasn't sure how she would feel when she did. Lila pushed the thought aside, reminding herself that this was about staying safe and hidden, not about rekindling an old flame.

The second floor had three spacious bedrooms that shared one bathroom. Lila took the middle bedroom, while Denise chose the one at the top of the stairs.

The crunch of wheels on gravel outside interrupted her thoughts. Lila stood up and walked over to the window, peering out through the blinds. A black SUV pulled up outside, and a figure climbed out, walking towards the cabin. It was Shane.

Lila felt her heart skip a beat as she watched him approach. He looked the same except for the scruff of beard. A five o'clock shadow that spoke of a day spent in travel. Where had he been? Had she pulled him from an assignment? She had to look at this as a business arrangement. Denise needed protection. *This isn't about Shane or me. It's about protecting Denise. Nothing more.*

"He's here."

Lila shoved the myriad of emotions she felt deep inside, walked down the stairs, and opened the door.

Reunion

-Shane-

Jack Benton's connections made travel easy. No cattle car seating on commercial flights, not with his varied financial holdings, including ownership, silent or otherwise, of several major airlines. Even when it wasn't work-related, Shane could simply call and schedule a flight wherever he wanted to go, first class. It was one perk of working for Benton Security Services.

He was the only one in first class. The back of the plane was perhaps half full, most of the others wore suits, and would get off at the first stop, New York, while he flew on to Bradley International, where a car was waiting for him.

The flight attendant was a familiar sight, although she wasn't usually on the red-eye. A willowy brunette, Dana had piercing green eyes and white teeth that she flashed in a megawatt-bright smile. Normally, she was on a regular daytime flight, not in the wee early morning hour shift. That was unusual. Over multiple trips, they had talked. She was his age, gorgeous and funny. She had given him her number four months ago. It had tempted him for a hot minute. But she had come along right after the break-up with Lila and he wasn't ready for anything, not even with the "no strings" that she scribbled on a napkin below her name and number.

"Shane Ellis, you are up early. Or is it a late night?" She asked, beaming.

"Hi Dana. Late night, I'm afraid. What are you doing on the red-eye?"

"Meeting my new boyfriend's family, actually. I'm attending his family reunion down in Texas with him."

"Sounds serious."

She giggled like a schoolgirl. "Yeah, it is. It took me by surprise. I didn't think I was cut out for anything long term. Not with my job. You know?"

Shit, yes, I know. My job screwed up my chances with Lila.

"I can certainly relate."

She nodded and then set a napkin down. "What can I get you?"

"Just a bottle of water, please. And a pillow. I think I'll try to catch some shuteye."

"Coming right up." She reached above him and turned off the light.

Shane allowed himself to relax. He tried not to think about what it would be like seeing Lila again. It had been six months, and still not a day went by that he didn't think about her, or worse, dream about her. His eyes closed, the sounds of other passengers trundling past with their suitcases lulling him to sleep. The plane taxiing to the runway barely registered, and he woke briefly as the plane left the ground and roared its way into the sky. When he opened his eyes hours later, there were only two more hours to go. He'd slept for nearly eight hours and felt refreshed, something that could not have happened were he stuck upright in the cattle car section of the plane.

He looked through the thick glass window at the bright blue sky. It was late morning by his estimate and the plane would land by 2:30, plenty of time to make the three-and-a-half-hour drive to the safe house. There had been closer airports, but Jack's reach, or that of the airlines he owned, while wide, did not go to every city in the country.

It was a pleasant drive. Plenty of scenic small towns along the way. Rural, with little changing in the past two hundred years. The picket fences and simple, well-built homes reminded him that some things lasted far longer than steel and concrete did on the west coast, especially in Los Angeles.

The safe house was new, and he had received access codes to it weeks ago when it came online. The photos he had seen of it shortly after they completed construction were nice, but it looked even better in reality. A sprawling, wood-shingle exterior with green-framed windows that let in light. They nestled it against a backdrop of forested land and set back from the road. Vaulted ceilings, wood-paneled walls, and three decent-sized bedrooms.

Custom-built, the windows were bulletproof and all doors, interior and exterior were steel-reinforced. A state-of-the-art security system was in place, as well as a panic room only accessible by fingerprint and retinal scan.

Ever since he had a near miss in his Los Angeles hills home, Jack made sure every one of his properties around the world, including the safe houses, were retrofitted, or built to order, to the new standards. Shane figured there was nothing quite like nearly being murdered in his own home to get serious about security. Shane suspected that Jack still felt bad about the Kansas City location not being updated at the time Shane and Lila were there two years ago. It had been further down on the list, and shortly after the shooting, Jack had it retrofitted.

Shane could see lights on inside. And movement. No great surprise, the driveway was long and winding, and he knew that Lila had followed safety protocols. Neither car was in sight and from the perimeter notifications he had received, she and this Denise Fortuna had arrived an hour ago. He had stopped for gas and bought some groceries. Fixings for dinner, and one of Lila's favorites, Chicken Piccata. Although he would have to make it with pasta, not the creamed polenta, and the country store had had no capers. Still, he was hoping an offering of a meal would smooth the way.

He had had most of a day to think of it, and he still couldn't figure out what to say, or do, to make things right between them. If it was even an option, which it didn't seem to be.

The last person I ever expected to talk to again.

It was on repeat in his head. She didn't want to give it another chance. How could she? She deserved better than a visit every few weeks or months. And the last one cut short by the call from Jack, demanding his return. She had only called him because she needed his help as a bodyguard, nothing more.

He could see the curtains move as he sat there in the car. She was waiting for him.

Waiting for me to come and do the only thing I'm good at. Stick to that, Ellis. Stick to your lane. Stop looking for more.

Shane sighed, shut the engine off, opened the door and stepped out from the car. His joints popped as he stretched, then reached for the bags of groceries and his go bag.

The door opened as he approached and Lila's beautiful face held a polite, perfunctory smile. "Thank you for this, Shane."

She took one bag from him and the door clicked shut behind them as he stepped inside.

All of his good intentions, the mental preparation he had made in the hours of travel, it all fell away. Just the sight of her was enough to undo six months of trying to convince himself that the two of them wouldn't work, couldn't. Shane wanted to reach out, pull her body against his, and kiss her. He wanted to feel her legs wrapped around his waist. He wanted tangled bedsheets, sweat, the scent of her hair.

Shane swallowed all of this down. Now was not the time. He set his bag on the entry floor, glanced at the young woman waiting nervously by the foot of the stairs, and did what he was supposed to do, what Lila needed from him, what she had asked of him.

"Of course. I'm Shane Ellis." He strode over to the young woman and extended his hand. "And you must be Denise."

"Y-yes." Denise said, her hand timid, limp in his.

"A pleasure to meet you. I've brought some fixings for dinner. Why don't I get started and after we eat, we can all talk about what comes next."

Undeniable

- Lila -

One day.

Two.

And now a third.

Damn it.

Lila could feel a hot flush creep over her. She'd tried to get over him. She was an educated, independent woman. So why was it whenever she was within ten feet of that arrogant muscled man, all she wanted to do was have him walk over, sling her over his shoulder like some damn cave man, and let him do wonderful, dirty things to her?

Get your mind out of the bedsheets, girl. The last thing you need is another roll in the hay with sexy, pecan pie Shane Ellis.

Shane cleared his throat. "Perhaps I should take over prepping the chicken."

Lila glared at him. "I know how to prep a chicken, Shane."

A ghost of a smile lifted the edge of his lips. "I know. It's just that..."

"What?"

"Well, you've been pounding that chicken with the mallet for five minutes now. At the rate you are going, it's going to be thinner than a tortilla." Lila glanced down at the chicken breast. She had pounded it flat.

He moved closer, his hand closing over hers. It was warm, and she felt a flush of desire slam into her.

If I feel like this when he simply puts a hand on me, how in the hell are we going to spend the next few days, or, heaven help me, weeks together?

"If you have some aggression to get out, might I suggest chopping some vegetables? Or would that be a bad idea to arm you with a knife?"

This close, she could smell him. It wasn't aftershave or cologne. Shane Ellis just smelled delectable. A mix of musk and sexy man reminded Lila of how long it had been.

Six months, three weeks, and two days, to be exact.

"Hand me a knife, then." Lila ground the words out.

He smiled, and removed his hand from hers, turned, and slipped a large knife into her free hand. She shuddered slightly, trying desperately to control her traitorous body and its runaway desire for the man next to her. She grabbed the head of broccoli and retreated to the far end of the kitchen island to work. It was close quarters, but she was better off creating space, any space, between her and Shane.

It's that or jump him and hump him like a sex-crazed dog.

"Are you cold?"

"What?" Lila responded, flustered.

"You shivered."

Why, oh why do even the simplest of words from him set me off? I just want to feel his hands wrap around my waist, cup my ass, slide me up against that wall, and...

"I'm fine." She said curtly. The knife sliced through the broccoli. Her knives at home were dull in comparison. This one sliced the broccoli as if it were nothing more than butter. She focused her intent on the broccoli, chopping away industriously at it, and trying desperately to avoid thinking of the man standing just a few feet away. Which wasn't so different from any of the hours, days, or weeks since she had told him they were over.

I can't stand it, the time apart. His job, his work, it isn't compatible with a relationship. This last year taught me that.

A mere moment passed before Shane was back at her side, his hand once again on hers.

For a man so invested in following The Code, he sure breaks the rules a lot.

"What now?" Lila barked, glaring up at him.

Why the hell did he have to be so tall, anyway?

"And now you have definitely ensured that any geriatric contingent of our group would have no problem consuming the meal."

"What?"

Lila followed his gaze down to the broccoli in front of her. She had devastated it, reduced the florets down to a fine mince. She had been so stuck in her own head that she hadn't even noticed.

"Oh."

She looked up at him, annoyed to see his lips twitch. Shane was clearly trying not to laugh.

The only thing the broccoli was good for now was, well, hell, she did not know. She had learned a handful of recipes from Shane. Mostly when he was in between assignments. They had either eaten out, or he had cooked while she wrote. The rest of their time together taken up with far more intimate, pleasurable pursuits. He pulled his hand away again and was at the refrigerator door.

He turned around, a small package in his hand. "Ah, this will work perfectly." He deposited a small square plastic-wrapped package in front of her.

"Wontons?" Lila read, "Like wonton soup?"

Shane had cooked her wonton soup the one time she came down with a miserable cold, thanks to a nasty virus making its way through town the past winter. It had been the next-to-last time he visited before she had broken it off.

"Actually, I'm thinking of fried wontons. It was one of my mom's comfort foods when I was growing up."

Lila blinked. Shane seldom spoke of his childhood. Both of their mothers had died of cancer, which seemed as if it would be something that they could speak candidly about, but Shane remained close-lipped about his life before he met Lila. He hadn't even really explained how he began working for Jack Benton as a bodyguard. *How did he describe it? A mistake that turned into an opportunity, one that he was lucky to get. Huh.*

It was yet another reason they couldn't work. She wanted to share everything, but Shane, well, he held a lot back. Why, she really didn't know. Whether it was a checkered past or a traumatic childhood, he wasn't willing to share. How could she think of the future with someone who avoided his past?

Shane tapped the top of the package. "Go ahead, open it up. And grab a ramekin and put some water in it."

"Ram-what?" Lila looked around the tiny kitchen.

Ram as in sheep? Why would I put water in sheep? Like, is that a cute name for sheep? Some sort of "love you, lambykins" kind of thing?

A white ceramic bowl appeared in front of her, his hand brushing hers. She felt another surge of lust and annoyance.

Oh. That's a ramekin?

She caught another grin from Shane. There and gone again, but his brown eyes twinkled with mischief.

It figures. He tells me to abide by the code and then does whatever the hell he wants. He's the one who keeps touching me!

The Code. Ugh. Cue the air quotes. As if The Code helped when the shit hit the fan last time.

It wasn't fair, though. Even as she thought it. She was the one who had opened the door to more danger. Using her phone had allowed the hitman to track her down there at the safe house.

Or maybe I'm jealous. Maybe he's interested in Denise now. Does protecting a woman make her somehow more attractive? Like some kind of macho man thing? Hell, maybe I'm still attracted to him. Of course I am, damn it, because why not be in a relationship with someone who simply cannot be here for me? I want him, but I want ice cream and junk food too. Just because I want something doesn't make it good for me.

His hand on her arm interrupted her thoughts again. "Are you okay?"

"Must you keep touching me?" The words popped out of her mouth before she could stop them. She glared up at him. He arched an eyebrow and his lips quirked into a trademark slow, sexy smile.

Standing there just as smug as can be.

"There should be a fifth rule." Lila added.

He blinked. "A fifth rule?"

"Of your stupid code. I think we need a rule that says, 'you shall not touch,'" Lila snapped. How in the world he expected her to stay calm with sexy pecan pie Shane Ellis standing so damned close, she did not know. It was impossible, the entire situation was impossible.

He laughed. Full throat guffaw. Lila could feel the heat rise in her cheeks.

"Jack would heartily approve of that rule."

He met her eyes, and Lila wasn't sure what she saw there. Was it desire? Frustration? Lust? Something more?

Shane opened his mouth, and Lila felt herself lean forward, wanting more than anything to hear what he would say next. Instead, his eyes flicked over her shoulder and past, to the doorway.

"Oh wow, I needed that. I really did," Denise said from the doorway, yawning as she stretched. "Did I get the best of the beds? It felt like I was sleeping on air." She blinked at the clock on the wall. "Is that clock right? Have I really been asleep for three hours?"

The moment between Lila and Shane was gone. Evaporated like mist. Whatever he started to say had disappeared into the ether.

It's better this way. After all, a couple of days and Jack will have someone else take over here. Shane will be gone and I can go back to my rental house and my bookstore, and Denise won't need my help anymore.

Still, the thought of saying goodbye to Shane left her with a cold, empty feeling in the pit of her stomach. For the hundredth time since she had called it off, whatever 'it' was between them, she felt the loneliness creep up and wrap itself around her heart.

We live far too different of lives to stay together. It won't work. It can't.

Lila smiled at her. "You definitely needed it. Do you mind helping Shane out? I think I'll go take a shower."

Denise nodded. "Oh yeah, for sure. I'd love to help."

Lila pointed to her spot in the kitchen and then marched upstairs to her en suite bathroom. She sighed, feeling conflicted. It was a relief to leave the kitchen. Being so close to him was harder than it should be. Why did he affect her so? Why did it have to be *his* touch that sent shivers through her body? Damn him. It felt as if her body didn't belong to her. It certainly did not obey her, not where Shane Ellis was concerned.

She thought about the differences between this safe house and the first one she had stayed in, trying to focus on anything else besides her ridiculous infatuation with the man downstairs.

The first safe house had been a study in contrasts - "the seventies have called and they want their flocked wallpaper back" had clashed with Victorian everything down to the dark, masterful Chesterfield sofa and chair that occupied the living room lined with wood parquet floors. This house was modern, yet with a rustic vibe. The toilet in the corner was also a bidet, and the controls on it seemed... *complicated*. She tugged her shirt over her head and reached into the shower, fiddling with it until she had one large showerhead, not all three, in action, before stripping off the rest of her clothes and stepping inside of it. The air conditioning kept the house cool, almost too cold, and Lila cranked the hot water up, fiddled with one of the other shower nozzles that dispensed a pulsating spray of heat into her lower back. This unfortunately reminded her of the hot tub at a wooded cabin deep in the forest. She'd gone away with Shane for a short two-day escape just as the fall was turning into winter. The nights had dipped below freezing, but the hot tub had been, well, hot. And in more ways than one. Thinking of that time with him, and the desires that ran through her body now, was stirring up so many emotions. Worse, her body was reacting to him. She felt as if she were no longer in control of it. Just being near him sent a curl of desire, heat, and more circulating through her.

I'm a hot mess around him. Maybe this was all a big mistake calling him. Perhaps I should have called Jack Benton directly, or stayed behind instead of coming with Denise.

The water pulsed into the small of her back. She reached for the shampoo and inhaled the scent of it. Sandalwood, musk, and peach floated into her nose. Shane baked a peach pie mid-summer when he had taken off for a long weekend last year. The shampoo brought the memory of it back, sharp. The taste of that pie, and the taste of it on his lips as he'd...

Get a hold of yourself, Lila!

But it was far too late. Now all she could think of were their stolen moments, scattered over the past year. Hands down, she had never, ever met a man who could satisfy her the way Shane had.

Mind-blowing sex, check.

Easy on the eyes, check.

Lila rinsed the last of the shampoo from her hair. Felt the suds slide down her body. Her hand strayed to that sensitive nub hidden in the now slick and sudsy folds. Overriding her better judgment, she allowed the memory of him standing before her, his mouth on hers. How he had pressed her against the cold tiles of the shower wall and worked his way down, ignoring the spray of the water by closing his eyes. His mouth sliding down to her breasts, taking one, then the other, gently nipping at them, before moving down her further, his hands sliding around to cup her ass and spread her legs apart just so.

Lila ran her finger along her clit, remembering how it had felt to feel his tongue questing, first gentle and barely there, to his mouth on her, his tongue slipping inside of her.

An orgasm ripped through her then, wringing a gasp of ecstasy from her lips. She felt the surge down to the tips of her toes as she stood there. A tremor rolled through her, the water cascading down over her head and pulsating into the small of her back, and then faded away. She came back to herself. A mixture of frustration and longing were all that remained in the aftermath.

This situation is impossible. I need to figure out what I want. And then I need to either leave and get on with my life, or...

Or what? Even she didn't know the answer to that.

Twenty minutes later, her hair damp, her body relaxed from the hot water, she returned to the common living area and breathed in the delicious aroma of dinner.

Denise was sitting on the couch, a troubled look on her face.

"What's wrong?" Lila asked, instantly concerned.

"It's my stomach. It just keeps acting up. The food was smelling so good and now..." Denise sat up suddenly, a look of panic on her face. She stood then and dashed past Lila, bolted into the half bath, and slammed the door. Lila could hear the faint sounds of retching.

She could feel Shane's presence behind her. Lila turned to face him. He frowned at the door, and then retching.

"Is she okay?"

They stood there listening as the toilet flushed and water ran in the sink.

Lila shrugged as her mind picked over the events of the past week. How many times had Denise been ill? This seemed excessive for a little stomach flu. A suspicion took root and grew. Lila opened her mouth to say something, but in that moment the door opened. Denise looked pale, distraught, her eyes filling with tears.

"Are you okay?" Lila asked. The girl looked like she needed a hug.

Denise shook her head. "I'm pretty sure I'm pregnant." And then she burst into tears.

What I Want

An hour later, Lila sat next to Denise, the pregnancy test Shane had brought back from the nearest convenience store sporting a plus sign on the table in front of them.

Dinner was a muted affair. Denise picked at her food, still pale, and managed only a few bites of the fried wontons before asking if there were any saltine crackers.

After the plates were cleared and Lila and Shane had cleaned the kitchen, Denise confirmed what they already suspected.

"It's his. It's Lionel's. I was on the pill and we, well, he, took no additional precautions past that. I thought the pill would be enough." She stared into the distance, one hand on her still-flat stomach.

Lila and Shane exchanged glances. This added a whole new level into an already complicated situation.

"Do you think he..." Lila paused, trying to find the words. "I mean..."

Denise snorted. Shook her head.

"I'm so stupid. He's rich, he's powerful, and..." Denise laughed bitterly, "And I have this sneaking suspicion that he's married, so..." She looked down at her stomach, fingers brushing at an invisible crumb. "So, I guess I, or *we*, are on our own." A moment of silence passed. "I'm keeping it. I figured someday I'd have a kid, maybe two. Maybe get lucky, meet a doctor, settle down." She laughed again, then shrugged, tears welling up in her eyes. "Instead, I got knocked up by a rich and powerful man who wants me dead."

Shane spoke first. "We don't know that these events are connected, not for sure."

Denise stared at him. "I told you what I overheard. What I certainly was *not* supposed to hear. And the next thing I know, someone has murdered my three friends. All for what? Being in the wrong place at the wrong time? It's connected, believe me. He's done having his fun, and now I'm a liability." She looked down at her belly again and placed one hand over it protectively. "*We* are a liability."

Shane folded his arms in front of his check, frowning, deep in thought. "Denise, I need to talk to my boss, Jack. He can help you, and Jack has contacts and resources I don't. I need to check in and see what our people have learned about this Lionel Bush, anyway."

Denise nodded absently. Her hand twisted in the cloth of her t-shirt. Shane stood up.

"I'll just step into the garage. Give Jack an update."

Lila watched him go, then focused on Denise. They sat in silence for a couple of minutes. If Lila listened closely, she could hear Shane's voice in the garage as he talked to his boss. But she couldn't hear what he was saying.

"I think that I'm going to go to bed. I'm just, I um, need to be alone if that's okay." Denise said apologetically. "I've got a lot to think about, you know?"

"Of course." Lila hadn't known Denise long, but she could tell the younger woman was struggling.

How would I feel in her shoes? She must be terrified. No support system. No partner and on the run from the father of her child.

"Denise." The younger woman stood up and looked back at her. "I promise we will do whatever we need to do to protect you and your child. Shane, and Jack, and the others. It's what they do. And they do their jobs well."

Denise nodded. She walked over to the stairs, put a hand on the rail and turned back to look at Lila. "Thank you. I know I've made my mess your mess somehow and I'm sorry for that."

"Don't be. We'll figure this out. Get some rest, okay?"

Denise nodded and disappeared upstairs, her bedroom door at the top of the stairs closing behind her with a gentle click.

Shane walked back in from the garage a few minutes later, sliding his phone into his pocket. He glanced around for Denise.

"She's gone up to her room," Lila said. "I think she needs time to process everything."

Shane nodded, looking grim. "Liam's dug up plenty. He's been updating me along with Jack. I didn't want to say anything until I had a solid picture of the situation."

"What did Liam find?" Lila knew Liam was some teenage wunderkind that worked for Jack while attending college. Shane was fond of the kid and impressed with the young man's hacking skills. He had mentioned him often.

"It was more of what he found *around* Lionel Bush. Disappearances. Deaths. Former employees who refuse to talk or just disappear. Family of missing employees asking questions and then going silent themselves. Nothing concrete. Nothing we can bring to the police, or the FBI even and say definitively that he's committed a crime. He's smart, he's rich, connected to some questionable organizations, and he's..." Shane stopped, his mouth set in a grim line. "He's dangerous, Lila."

Lila felt a heavy dread forming in her chest. "Why do terrible people always get away with things? When do we get a chance to live without looking over our shoulder all the time?" Anger warred with the dread. Her situation wasn't any different. The powers behind Kurgen Real Estate, the hints of a secret crime syndicate, all of it. It had exploded her life, her chances at a normal existence. "I write under a pen name, have to remember to respond to 'Annie' when I'm in a crowd. I'm stuck in WitSec, waiting for a trial that might never happen. When do I get to live a normal life? And Denise? With a baby on the way? When does she get to feel safe?"

Shane reached out and pulled her against him. For the first few seconds, she felt hard, brittle, and so angry. She fought the temptation to lash out, to hit Shane. Her life had been upended. Denise and what she was going through was just yet another reminder of it.

"Hey." Shane said softly, "Breathe. Just... breathe."

This close to him, his body was warm, and the hot, moist air in the garage clung to his kin. His breath tickled the top of her head. He smelled of soap and the faintest hint of the lemongrass-scented shampoo the bathrooms were stocked with. His touch was reassuring, calming.

Lila felt her stress slipping away and replaced by something else, an attraction she wished she could fight, but had no genuine interest in doing so. Here in Shane's arms, no matter that they were in the middle of nowhere in some safe house, here she felt safe and... wanted.

What do I want from him? Another quick whirlwind of amazing food, sex, and then... what? I want him. I wish I didn't. I wish I was cool with just casual sex. That I could just...

Shane's voice interrupted her inner monologue. "Hey, where is your head at? I can feel you tensing up all over again."

His words tickled her ear and sent a wash of hedonistic desire down her spine. She didn't bother fighting it. She couldn't. It felt as if she and Shane were made for each other. The way their bodies moved together or the attraction they both felt. The sex. God, the mind-blowing sex.

She knew the choice was there. Step back, break the connection or move closer, consummate the desire thrumming there in the air, and coiling inside of both of them. She knew he wanted her just as much as she wanted him. It was there, unspoken, but real. And even as her mind gibbered questions of how they would make it work, what disaster this could bring, she melted into him, one hand on his chest, the other clenched in a fist. She gripped his t-shirt, pulled him down toward her, and tilted her head up to capture his mouth in hers.

His mouth crashed into hers. The months of being alone with only the memory of him, the frustration over his job, their lack of quality time together, it all melted away as their tongues entwined. As if they shared the same thoughts, Shane lifted her easily into his arms and strode toward the stairs, never breaking from the kiss. God, how she had missed this feeling. The feel of a man who could hold her, carry her up a flight of stairs without breaking a sweat. It felt as if she blinked twice and they were at his door, through it, and he set her on the edge of his bed, a hungry look in his eyes.

All the doubts, the hurt, the frustration - she pushed them aside. She wanted him and he wanted her, and really, what more was there than this moment, right now? Life can turn on its ear in a second, and everything you had or thought you wanted can be ripped away.

This is real, and this is what I want.

Shane nodded and Lila realized she had said it out loud. He knelt down in front of her, keeping eye contact as he slipped her t-shirt off, revealing the white lace bra underneath. His hand lit a fire inside her as he slid one, then the other bra strap down and bent to kiss, then gently nibble and suck at her breasts. Pleasure coursed through Lila and she leaned back on his bed, closed her eyes, and moaned. He continued his way down her body. His hand slid slowly, possessively, down her front, to the waist of her capris, past the waistband, plunging toward her hot depths. His mouth gave both pleasure and pain as he took first one breast than the other in his mouth, his tongue rolling over each sensitive nipple before nipping them lightly.

He slipped her pants off, and tossed them away, his hand already back against her mons, a finger slipping expertly inside the hot, slick folds. Lila moaned, clutched the bedding between her fingers, and fell back as Shane moved sensuously down her body, his mouth trailing kisses from her breasts down her breastbone, to her navel, and then slipping his fingers inside of her, his warm breath sent shivers across her skin.

The terrible and wonderful things his fingers and mouth were doing to her sent flashes of light across her closed eyes. It felt as if he had unleashed lightning in her bloodstream. Lila wanted to lose herself in the sensation.

"Come for me." Shane said, staring up at her, his tongue and mouth sparking a lightning storm inside of her. Then he did something with his fingers and there was no more thought, only sensation and light. Her body was on fire as an orgasm exploded through her.

Later, much later, after their bodies had come together in a frenzy of lovemaking, Shane curled his body around her. One arm underneath, curling over her possessively, his fingers stroking her skin. "Your skin feels like silk." He murmured in her ear. It tickled, but Lila was far too exhausted to wiggle away.

"What are we going to do about Denise?" she asked, yawning. Her body felt like a limp puddle after two mind-blowing orgasms.

"Jack will be here in the morning. He's got some ideas."

Oh great. Lila knew she should be thankful for Jack Benton. He had done plenty for her, and all with no payment. Although Shane had explained that the jobs he often took were the ones that paid for the other cases like hers, she still felt like she owed Jack Benton something. And she didn't like feeling indebted to anyone, not even a billionaire like Benton.

Besides, Benton is the reason Shane and I broke up. If Jack would have just honored Shane's time off, we...oh hell, who am I kidding? It was only a matter of time. I'm not made for long-distance relationships, or ones where I'm alone for weeks at a time. I know this.

As if sensing her displeasure, Shane said, "He's a good guy, Lila. One of the best I know."

Lila sighed. Damned if he couldn't read her mind.

"I know. And I'm *grateful*, really, I am. It's just..." Even now, they would not agree. She knew this. Shane felt he owed Benton, and maybe he did. All Lila knew was that she really didn't want to wait around for the bits and pieces that were left.

"It's just that you want more. You want me around, not off on assignment." Shane rumbled in her ear, finishing her sentence.

Lila flipped over, faced him. "Is that so wrong?"

"No, it absolutely isn't." He met her eyes, steady, unblinking. "And I'm trying to figure out how to make it all work. Maybe I can ask Jack to only give me work in the Northeast region, so I'm closer."

Lila felt the conflicting emotions bubble up. Shane was trying, at least, to make it different. But would it be that different? Close or far, it wasn't as if he could drive home every night. Gone, whether it was an hour's drive or half a continent, was still gone. She wanted to say it was enough, that they could make it work, but the nature of his work was the issue. Days, weeks, even months away on assignment. She'd never been a Tinder kind of girl. More of an eHarmony one. Once, back in Kansas City, she had signed up for it after Kaylee's persistent nagging. She'd met a couple of bland, run-of-the-mill guys, another weird one who gave off stalker-like vibes, before she'd connected a guy who met all her basic criteria. He also turned out to be in the military. She'd wrestled over it for a good part of a day, before turning down a second date. She wasn't interested in a military life. A friend in high school had grown up a military brat. She and Lila had been fast friends for the second half of ninth grade and then lost touch once the girl's father was assigned to a new post on the east coast.

And really, was this situation any different? Shane might as well be in the military. Days, weeks, months away from home and facing all kinds of situations and danger.

No thanks. I'd rather live alone.

"Lila?" Shane's voice intruded on her thoughts. "What are you thinking about?"

"Don't you want something different, Shane?"

"Different from what?"

"You know, different. You live out of a duffel bag. Your pistol and ammo take up more room in it than your socks do."

"I don't need much of anything." He said in response, his body tensing.

"What about us? Don't you want more for *us*? And don't you dare tell me how good Jack has been to you and how much he depends on you. He's a *billionaire*. He pays enough that he could buy whatever loyalty he needs five times over if you left. You know, you could go back to medical school, become the doctor you dreamed of being."

"Doctors are gone long hours, Lila. Even if I could get back into medical school, any internship would have me working 80 hours a week or more."

"At least you would come home every day! And you wouldn't have someone shooting at you," Lila snapped back, frustrated. She sat up abruptly. She knew where this was going.

What I want is a partner, someone to spend my days and nights with. And Shane will not be that for me. Not now, and maybe never.

She reached for her clothes. They were scattered across the room. A bra here, a pair of panties over there.

"Where are you going?"

"To my bed. This was a mistake." And before Shane could argue, she slid out of the door and closed it firmly behind her.

No Way to Prove It

- Lila –

Lila woke to the sunlight streaming in the window. It was a beautiful morning, at odds with her current frame of mind. Would anything she had said sway Shane? Could she even hope for him to show a spine to his boss?

He's not spineless. He's... devoted. But I wish he were a little less devoted. I really do.

She could hear sizzling sounds coming from the kitchen. The smell of coffee had wafted under her door, gently tempting her from her bed. No doubt it was Shane. The man was a wizard in the kitchen and in the bedroom. She groaned, pulling the sheet back over her face, wishing it was just the two of them in her rental house in Maine. Wishing she knew how she could make it work between her and Shane.

Today Jack Benton would be here. She hoped he had some miraculous solution for Denise's predicament. All Lila wanted to do was flee back to her bookstore and her life, single and lonely as it might be.

Two hours later, Jack Benton sat down across from Denise, who fidgeted and paced restlessly until Lila settled into a seat next to her.

"I wish I could tell you that the good guys always win." Jack said. "But that simply isn't the case." He tapped the folder on his lap. "My people dug up a lot. But none of it will stick. Not without more witnesses, a smoking gun, *something*. A judge will throw this out in an instant."

"What about evidence of medical testing?" Lila asked. "Surely someone could investigate that, find out if there have been any victims or deaths as a result?"

Jack shook his head. "We are looking into it, but honestly? Liam has found nothing so far. We'll keep trying, but until we have evidence, no one is going to believe it. The Happy Haven Retirement Villages are popping up everywhere, and they are revolutionizing senior care."

"My friends are dead. The police are hunting *me* and plastering *my* face all over the news and there's nothing I can do?" Denise said, her thin, strained. She pulled her legs up against her, wrapped her arms around herself, and rocked her body back and forth. "My life has been destroyed. My reputation, my future as a nurse. I can't go back to Florida, I can't even go back to Maine. I can't even be a nurse without documentation from my college. What in the hell do I do?"

Jack nodded and placed a business card on the coffee table, sliding it over until it sat within reach of Denise. She stared at it. "What's this?"

"I made a few calls before I left California. His name is Doc Diamond. He needs a nurse." Jack said.

"Who is this guy, really?" Denise asked, peering at the card.

"He's a well-qualified, brilliant doctor. I can tell you that. He got caught up in a family member's mess and the cops pinned a crime on him he didn't commit. He is offering you the full package, income, health insurance, paid leave, annual bonuses, and no questions asked. And we can make sure you have a new identity. Doc Diamond operates out of southern California, and he caters to those who don't want or need their medical needs leaked to the public. The rich, and others, not-so-rich, who are afraid of immigration."

Jack leaned forward. "This is only temporary, Denise. Consider it a stepping off point to your new life. One that establishes your employment history by giving you the necessary experience. In a few years, you can find something else in a smaller town. There are plenty throughout the west coast, but I have a couple in mind that I could get you a position in when one opens up."

"But... how?" Denise turned the card over in her hands, a frown on her face, "I mean, how can you make it look right, or authentic? Will it even hold up if I get pulled over? Or will I be in worse trouble?"

Jack smiled. His teeth were a brilliant white. "Money buys a lot of things, Denise. It buys silence. It buys zero questions, new identities, and plenty more. But don't worry, I use my powers for good."

She was still frowning. "And what will this cost me? I mean, I don't have money to pay you."

Jack shook his head. "I don't need payment. Or favors. Or for you to owe me. This is what I do." He templed his long, manicured fingers in front of him as if in supplication. "Some day, you will find someone to help, just as Lila helped you. You pay it forward however you can, when you can. I just hope that we can get enough on this Lionel Bush, and on Happy Haven for you to reclaim your life someday. For now, however, you can have a decent go at a different one. Is that acceptable?"

"I'll really be able to work as a nurse?"

"You will."

"Am I going to be working for the mob or gangsters?" She asked, apprehension clear from the frown on her face.

Jack smiled and shook his head. "No. Doc Diamond handles some celebrity cases, and a handful of those who might skirt the law, and I and others supplement his work with immigrants afraid to use the health care system, but it is a rare day Doc caters to organized crime. If he did, you could bow out of caring for any patient who made you uncomfortable. There is another nurse on his staff. He simply wanted to add a second. He mentioned it, and I thought immediately of you."

There was a moment of silence before Denise nodded slowly. "Okay. Yes, I would be interested."

"Excellent." Jack pulled out his phone and made a call. "Az? Tell Liam I'll need the full package. I'll fly back with her today. And reach out to Doc and tell him she can start next week. Yes. And the apartment in L.A. is vacant, right? Great. Set up access to that and a commuter car. Thanks." He pressed a button and slid the phone into his jacket pocket.

"I've included a place to stay. The apartment has two bedrooms and is in a secure building. There's parking as well and my assistant, Azule, is making all the arrangements for access to a no-frills, but reliable, car. The apartment and the car are payment-free for two years, enough time for you to get on your feet, have your child, establish credit under your new identity, and more. If you need something further, keep my card and simply reach out to me." He slid a plain card across the coffee table.

There was a long pause. Lila itched to say something about how it had been for her. Although WitSec, for what they were worth, had been involved, and it had been a completely unique experience, she knew how hard it was. You had to let go of the life you had lived and embrace another. At least Denise could use her education, something she trained for.

I wish I could have continued in data analysis, if only because it feels like I wasted years studying for it, only to end up in a completely different field. Still, I love the opportunities I have now.

Lila cast a glance in Shane's direction. He said little at breakfast other than to tell them that Jack Benton was on his way and would be there soon. It felt as if he'd been deliberately avoiding her. As if they were back to square one again. Even Denise, her mind full of her own problems, had noticed.

"What's with your hunky guy?" Denise had asked earlier, when Shane had slipped out of the door to walk around the property before Jack arrived.

"What makes you think he's mine?" Lila had asked in return, a surge of bitterness rising in her.

Denise had raised an eyebrow and snorted. "Maybe the way he looks at you like you are the only person in the world that matters? If I had a guy look at me like that, well, I wouldn't kick him out for eating crackers in bed if you know what I mean." She'd stopped and stared at Lila. "Oh my God, this is the sexy pecan pie guy from your novel, isn't it?"

"Yeah, well..." Lila had struggled with what to say, what to share.

"Write what you know?" Denise had giggled then, momentarily distracted from the morning sickness that had kept her from finishing the eggs and toast Shane had prepared.

Lila had laughed wryly and shrugged. "I guess so."

"Sex must be..."

"Epic with a side of 'now I'm leaving on assignment and I don't know when I'll be back,'" Lila finished, shoving her half-eaten breakfast away from her. She'd lost her appetite. "Also, 'you don't understand, I *owe* him my freedom, I can't just leave him in a lurch.'" She had added finger quotes in the air, her tone sounding bitter.

"Oh." Denise had practically wilted in her seat. "That..."

"Sucks. Yeah, I know." Lila had shrugged. "We got close again, had the same conversation, and now we are back where we started."

It was hard to even look at him. Part of her wanted to just rip off her clothes and fuck some sense into him, and the other part wanted him to look at her, realize how much he needed her and tell that silver fox, Jack Benton, to take his job and shove...

"Ms. Benoit." Speaking of silver foxes, Jack's gaze was now focused entirely on her.

"Um, what?"

Jack's mouth quirked to one side in amusement. "I asked how the bookstore and book writing is coming."

Coming? I have my characters coming all over the place.

"Um, fine, fine. Yeah. Uh, eager to get back to it."

"Well, Kaylee asked me to tell you she is looking forward to the next installment."

Lila gaped at him. "You are in contact with Kaylee?"

Jack's smiled deepened. "We reconnected when she reached out to me to get you protection. And, well, we've been together ever since."

Lila struggled to close her mouth. Her mind spun. *Kaylee and Jack? And here I had chalked him up as a billionaire playboy!*

She leaned toward him. "Is there a way, I mean, is it safe to call her? WitSec told me not to contact anyone from my past, and really, except for Kaylee, there wasn't anyone to contact. But if she's with you..."

Jack nodded, pulled a pen from his pocket, and jotted down a phone number. "I know she would love to hear from you. We all run with Purism Librem smartphones. They are untraceable." He slid his card across the table, a phone number written neatly at the bottom.

"Thank you. I'll call her soon." Excitement surged through her, replacing her disappointment and frustration with hope. Kaylee had always known exactly what to say or do with dating and relationships, and fashion, and more. Lila had missed her vivacious friend more than words could express. She missed late night pizza runs in the middle of study sessions, lunches at Nara when they were both working at Kurgen, and the First Fridays jaunts between Christopher Elbow Chocolates and Mean Mule Distillery. Kaylee embodied everything Lila missed of Kansas City, and her former life.

"Well," Jack said, clapping his hands together. "I think that wraps everything up. I'll escort Ms. Fortuna back to California."

"How will I get through airport security?" Denise asked, worry creasing her forehead.

"I have a private jet waiting for us in Laconia," Jack answered. He nodded at Shane. "You can head back to Alaska if you like, or elsewhere," his gaze strayed to Lila, "I don't have a new assignment for you yet."

Lila blinked. That was as close to a tacit approval of her and Shane's relationship as she had ever seen. Too bad it came months too late.

Jack turned back to Denise. "I'd like to leave soon. We have a long flight ahead of us and by midday, the queue for the runway can get rather long."

Denise nodded and stood. "I just need to gather my things and I can be ready in ten minutes."

Jack Benton smiled at her, nodded at Lila, and called after Denise as she walked up the stairs. "I'll be in the car waiting."

As Denise disappeared into her bedroom to pack, Lila stood as well. "Thank you, Jack, for everything." Somehow, knowing he was with Kaylee made him feel less like an adversary, and more like an ally. She still wished Shane would give his notice, choose a life with her instead, but knowing she could speak to her friend was an unexpected bonus.

Who knows, maybe Kaylee can help me figure this whole mess out. Or set me straight, hell maybe even tell me to dump Shane.

"Happy to help." Jack answered. He gazed up the stairs, then turned back to Lila. "I wish I had better answers for her, but connecting the fire and murders to Lionel Bush is impossible. Perhaps if they catch up with the one who actually did the deed, we can convince them to talk. Until then, well, the police will not see Ms. Fortuna as a victim in this situation. And worse, they cannot protect her."

Lila sighed and rubbed her face. "That sure sounds familiar."

Jack nodded. "If this were a movie, karma would catch up to the bad guys and rain down retribution on them. And believe me, I want to see that happen, Ms. Benoit, I do. You and Ms. Fortuna are being hunted by people who wish to do you harm, but we are also stalking our prey. If we can connect enough dots, we can bring them down. Give Liam time. He's working on it. So is Azule. Together, they make a rather formidable team."

Lila smiled at Jack's comment. Shane had mentioned both Liam and Azule often. Liam was still in his teens, but Shane described him as a converted black hat hacker. The kid had skills and had lived in Kansas City until he tracked Jack down and quickly made himself indispensable. Apparently, he was now living at Jack's estate and attending college while also handling anything computer-related. Then there was Azule, a competent, smart black woman a few years younger than Jack. She had grown up on the Benton estate while her parents worked for Jack's parents and began working for Jack once she had finished college. She was Jack's personal assistant, and ruled the office with an iron fist, according to Shane, who described her as "formidable."

It felt anti-climactic. Denise would get a new life, a new identity, although it differed considerably from Lila's experience. Denise was being sought by the police, hunted by a powerful man. Lila, at least, had been protected by WitSec, who she probably should update about all the goings on over the last few days. Especially with the hurricane hitting the entire North Atlantic seaboard, they might be a little concerned.

Or not. And talk about a case going nowhere. My case is going nowhere. Kind of like this off again, on again relationship with Shane.

"Well, it sounds like Denise is in excellent hands." She smiled to cover up the rush of depression that flooded her. "I guess I need to pack my bags as well. And get on the road if I want to make it back to Brunswick before nightfall. I have a bookstore to run." Lila said. She avoided looking at Shane, who had been sitting in an armchair a few feet away. She fixed her gaze on Jack. "Thank you again for this. I can't tell you how much I appreciate all that you are doing for Denise, and what you did for me as well."

She knew Jack Benton had been involved in setting up the bookstore for her, despite WitSec and the FBI being in charge of her case. Shane had admitted as much. Jack Benton had done a lot for her. And seeing him again reminded her of that. It gave her a new understanding of *why* Shane was so loyal. Jack protected people. He didn't make money on it, at least, not all the time. In fact, she suspected he probably operated Benton Security Services at a loss. It seemed that Jack continued to defy the stereotypical playboy billionaire image. Why, she wasn't sure.

I'll bet there is a story there, though.

It didn't make the situation between her and Shane any better – she still wanted a partner by her side, not this part-time thing they had – but at least she could see *why*.

"I'm happy I could help, Ms. Benoit." Jack answered.

Lila turned and headed for the stairs without looking at Shane. She could feel his eyes on her the entire way up the staircase. When she turned at the top and looked, his eyes met hers, his shoulders slumped. Her chest felt tight as she turned away and went into her room.

It took moments to pack, and another five to say goodbye to Denise, who teared up and hugged her.

"Thank you, Lila. I don't know what I would have done without your help."

Lila hugged her back. "You are going to be okay, Denise. And you will soon have a beautiful baby to keep your heart and hands full. I hope you will keep in touch."

The house will feel empty without Denise there.

Denise promised she would, hugged Lila again, and pulled away, wiping at the tears on her cheeks. As Lila turned to go, Denise put a hand on her shoulder, "I hope you work things out with pecan pie guy."

Lila laughed, gathered her bags, and headed downstairs.

Shane stood. "Let me walk you out."

Lila nodded and said, "Thank you again, Jack. And if you could let Kaylee know I'll try to call her while I'm on the road, I'd appreciate it."

"Will do." Jack answered as Shane picked up the heavier suitcase and slung Lila's duffel bag over his shoulder.

The door closed behind them. The heat of the summer day was just beginning to build.

"Lila, I feel like we left things unsaid last night."

"No, I don't think we did, Shane." She popped the back trunk lock and Shane slid both bags into it.

"Lila..."

"Shane. Let's just say goodbye, okay?" Lila didn't want to cry in front of him. She just wanted to smile and get out of here before the waterworks started. She'd cry on the road, call Kaylee, pour out her heart, and get past this. "I get it, I really do. What Jack does, the people he helps, that's important. It's meaningful. He's changing lives. And you are a part of that."

"Yes, but..."

"I'm going to go now." She could feel the tears threatening, and damned if she wanted to do it in front of Jack or Denise or even Shane. And before he could try to change her mind, she gave him a chaste kiss on the cheek, slipped into the driver's seat, and pulled out of the garage, leaving Shane standing there. She reversed, turned around in the wide driveway, and pulled away. She couldn't help thinking how forlorn he looked in the rearview as she drove away.

Where is She?

- Lila -

Returning home, or the equivalent thereof, after the last few days in the safe house, felt off, weirdly foreign, despite missing all of her belongings and familiar space. The hurricane had blasted through and left trees down; the electricity had been out, and from the smell coming from the fridge, it had been at least two days without power. She had been so distracted by Denise, and her reunion with Shane, that Lila hadn't realized how bad the storm had been until she arrived at the dark house.

On the door was a note, unsigned, telling her the bookstore had sustained damage. A broken window, possibly flooding. Lila groaned. She'd spent hours on the road driving home, had to prove she lived in the town in order before the guys in uniform at the edge of town would let her through the barricades, and now she would need to go to the bookstore and assess the damage.

I wish Shane was here.

She wrenched the car into drive and reached for her phone. The battery was red-lining, despite being plugged into the charger the entire drive home. She followed the cable to the plug, and it wiggled, loose, unconnected.

Well, shit. I ran it down while talking to Kaylee for so long. Damn it.

At that moment, it rang and she could see Shane's sexy mug staring up at her. Lila pressed the green button.

She tried to keep her voice noncommittal. They were done. She needed to get over it, get over him. "Hey."

"I tried calling earlier, but it kept going to voicemail. I was getting concerned."

"I was on the phone with my friend Kaylee."

"Oh." He paused, then asked, "Did you make it home yet?"

"I did. But now I have to run to the bookstore. There's damage from the storm. They left a note on my door."

"I can be there to help. I'm approaching some roadblock right now. When you didn't answer, I took a detour."

A four-hundred-mile detour? Really?

Lila sighed. "Really, it will be okay. I can handle it." She backed out of the driveway, neatly avoiding a fallen branch.

"Lila, I..."

"Look, Shane, there's really nothing more to say. You have your work, and I have a life here. What more is there to talk about?"

He fell silent. The only way she knew he was there was his breathing and the sounds of the occasional honk.

He really did take a detour. By now, he should be halfway back to Alaska! Then again, Jack had practically encouraged him to do so. As if he had a change of heart. Maybe Kaylee had said something to him. She'd certainly been supportive when they talked.

"Girl, it sounds like the two of you could really make something beautiful together." Those had been Kaylee's words after Lila poured her heart out. "But yeah, I have to agree, it would be impossible as a long-distance relationship. It was why I cut it off with Jack. He was in California; I was in college and then Kansas City. It was just too much." Her voice had softened then, "But seeing him again, Lila, in the middle of all the Kurgen shit that went down, I just... I don't want to ever be apart from him again."

"Lila, are you still there?" Shane asked, jostling her back to the present.

"Yep, just trying to drive around all the storm damage."

"So, what do you think?"

"About what?" Lila asked, momentarily confused.

"I asked if I could swing by the house, make you dinner."

Debris cluttered the intersection, and the signal lights were dark, lifeless. Thankfully, most of downtown Brunswick was closed thanks to the power outage. She waited for a truck to cross through the intersection and then turned right onto the side street behind the bookstore.

"There's no power." Lila answered.

"It's a gas stove. I can light it manually. Besides, I'd feel better if I just double-checked the house. Denise created a trail, cash withdrawals from the bank. If Lionel Bush hired a hit on her, he's got the same resources for tracking her down that we do, possibly more. Let me just look at the house, cook you something, and we could, you know, talk."

I can think of much more pleasurable activities than talking. Damn it. NO. No talking. Talking leads to... other things. Far more pleasurable to be sure, but what we need is to just... stop.

"I don't think that's a good idea." Lila said, hating how indecisive and weak her voice sounded. Damn Shane Ellis. He knew just what buttons to push.

I'm so damned predictable. Feed me wonderful food, turn those sexy brown eyes in my direction and my legs open like a...

"I just can't stop thinking about you. About us. I don't want this to be over."

In the background, she could hear someone shouting from another car. It had taken her an hour in line on the outskirts of town to get through. The hurricane had been a doozy from the looks of it. And most of the town had fled, and was only now returning. Tempers were flaring as the National Guard took its time looking up resident addresses and double-checking the occupants' identities.

She could also feel her will weakening. Hope threading through after talking with Kaylee and hearing in her friend's voice how in love she obviously was.

The silver fox and Kaylee. What a world. There had to be at least a decade between them, but if it works for Kaylee, and she is happy, who am I to judge?

And maybe, just maybe, she should give it one last chance. Lila drew in a lungful of breath, let it out, and relented.

"Okay."

"Yeah?" She could see his smile, hear it in his voice.

"Yeah. I've got some wood in the back of the bookstore. I'll get it up against the window, move some books..."

"I can be there in ten to help. I'm almost at the front of the line."

"See you soon," Lila said, and the phone beeped and went black.

Dead as a doornail. Damn it.

She had circled the block. All the buildings were dark, the power was down throughout the town. Trees and debris still filled the streets. From the boards covering the other buildings, including Hannifords, it seemed the hurricane had mostly spared the businesses. The shrubbery and trees were the exception to this, and her bookstore, of course. She hadn't been here to add that spare wood to the front of the building in time. It was no wonder downtown was deserted. Most of the store owners were probably intent on cleanup at home. Lila spotted a parking space clear of debris at the front of the bookstore and pulled in and parked.

Her stomach churned in anticipation at seeing Shane again. It had only been a few hours, hours she had spent mostly on the phone, catching up with Kaylee. Still, a tiny thread of hope bloomed inside her.

He sounded so earnest. And he followed me four hours out of his way.

She turned off the engine, opened the door, and slid out of the car. There, near the front door, the glass was shattered, a long, battered tree branch lying half in, half out of the long glass show window. Several books, her thrillers and beachside cozies, lay sprawled willy-nilly underneath it, the covers and pages swollen with rain, the rest of the display case scattered in the wind. Lila sighed.

Really, it isn't as bad as I thought it would be. I think I got off lucky.

The door was unlocked. That raised Lila's eyebrows, but only for a moment, before she laughed out loud.

"I guess no one is as crazy for books as I am," she said out loud and pushed open the door. The bell jingled as the door scraped against broken glass.

The light of the day, already murky and hidden behind heavy cloud cover, was rapidly fading. She could make out the bookshelves and most of the main room, but the back office remained shrouded in darkness.

I could just wait for Shane. She eyed the dark outline of the closed office door. *Yeah, like a helpless ninny. No thanks. I can at least get the board out and ready for when he's here to help.*

She picked up the stack of damaged books and set them out of the way. Lyle, Hanniford's owner, had delivered the boards just days before the storm. It was one of the few things she appreciated about living in a small town. People looked out for each other, even newcomers like Lila. When she had looked confused at his offering, he had explained what they were for.

"So's your windows don't get blown out by the hurricane."

And she had planned on putting up the wood. Until that newscast and Denise's face plastered all over it. Three days, no, four, and it felt more like a month.

Suddenly, the thought of Shane on his way to the bookstore felt like a bad idea all over again.

I'll get the board up over the broken glass, clean up, and by the time he gets here, I'll just tell him to go. I can't keep doing this to myself, wanting what I can't have.

She picked her way past a pile of books, victims of the wind, all cozy mysteries, and headed for the back of the store. She knew right where it was, near the back wall next to a new shipment of children's books she had meant to ask Denise to shelve, but they had instead had to deal with a flurry of visitors intent on buying books to read during the upcoming storm. Lila opened the office door and stepped into the darkness. It smelled of paperbacks, books that were likely suffering in the humid heat left in the hurricane's wake. A small, barred window high on the wall was the only light source, and a rapidly fading one at that. There was some other, odd smell that hit Lila at around the same time as something slammed into the side of her, jabbering as it did, knocking her to the ground. Pain flared, pinpoints of electric pain, her muscles contracting without her consent, her mind momentarily knocked offline. Consciousness lost.

Someone dragging her by her hair, a sharp ache of agony from her scalp. She opened her mouth to scream and the man, it was a man, growled, "Scream and I'll kill you. Right here. Right now."

He crouched over her, a dark blocky figure that removed the light from the room. He pressed a hard object to her abdomen. It felt small, round, barrel-shaped. Lila's heart hammered in her chest.

"Where is she?"

"Wh...wh...who?" Lila stammered, desperate to buy time. How long would it take Shane to get through the roadblock? Could they even let him through? He wasn't a resident. She'd had to prove it, show her driver's license that listed her address. They might turn him away, even detain him if he argued.

"Denise Fortuna. Your employee. Your roommate. Do not play dumb with me." The man said. His breath stunk. It smelled of something familiar.

Shane. Oh God, Shane. I need you here. Now!

Even if they let him through, how long would it take him to get here? Five minutes? Maybe even ten?

When seconds count...

The man jabbed the gun harder against her skin. It jabbed painfully against the bottom of her left ribcage.

This close, I'll be dead, bled out, long gone, before anyone can get me to a hospital.

"Where... is... she?"

Lila's mind gibbered in fear. Her hand, lost in the shadows, closed on the Taser he had used to debilitate her. She slid it into her waistband.

If I tell him the truth, he'll kill me. If I lie, tell him she's at the house, he will kill me.

Somehow, she had to stay alive. She had to stay alive long enough for Shane to get there. Her mind spun.

"I can take you to her."

The gun jabbed her again, bruising, painful. "I want the address."

Give him an address and I'm dead.

Lila shook her head. "I... don't..." he jabbed her again. "I don't know the address. It was just... everyone was leaving, but Denise was sure you would find her, that you already knew what her car looked like, so we dumped her car at an airport, backtracked."

He reached up with his free hand, grabbed a handful of her hair, and twisted hard. Tears sprang to her eyes.

"We... we hid on the outskirts of town. I can... I can show you. Just please, please don't hurt me." She was sobbing now. It wasn't hard. She was terrified. Despite the moist heat, her limbs trembled, still reeling from the spasms.

He's got a gun and a Taser. Hit me with the Taser first. So where is the Taser?

"Get up."

Doritos. He smells of Cool Ranch Doritos.

The random fact popped into her brain. She stocked her desk drawer with the variety snack packs. Cool Ranch Doritos were ones she saved for last. Her favorite.

Fucker ate my Doritos!

She felt a flare of ridiculous and rather misplaced anger at the thought. But somehow, being angry was better than being scared. She had been so frightened that, if she had not run out of water miles ago, and stopped to use the restroom before coming to the bookstore, there would be an embarrassing puddle on the floor of her office right now. Angry felt more focused. Anger would keep her alive.

He yanked her to her feet by her hair. He was tall, a hair taller than Shane, and brutal. The darkness of the room and her prone position on the floor had kept his face hidden, but now, on her feet, she could see more details. This was a very dangerous man. There was no room for error, no way to fight, not with the gun held close against her body. Her head ached from where he had wrenched her hair, and she was sure he had pulled some of it out at the roots.

His bad breath, tinged with the hint of Cool Ranch Doritos, washed over her. "Try anything, and I'll fucking kill you."

Lila's stomach lurched in revulsion and terror. She thought of the man she had shot in the basement of Jack Benton's safe house. That had been simple. The hitman hadn't even known she was there. She had squeezed the trigger, half out of reflex, as he turned toward her. She knew she had been lucky, damned lucky. This situation was different. He was too close. She couldn't run and she didn't dare try to fight him. She was a fool to have even done what she had, grabbing that Taser. What if her shirt didn't cover it? What if he remembered he should have it?

He spun her around, shoved the barrel of the gun Into her side with one hand, and wrapped the other in her hair at the nape, twisting it painfully as he did.

"You parked out front. If there is anyone there, if you scream, fight, try to run, know I will kill you and anyone who gets in my way. Understand?"

"Y-yes." She hated how tiny and helpless her voice sounded. She wished she was brave, that she wasn't so damned scared right now.

They moved slowly out of the office, into the gloom of the bookstore, then out the front door. The bell jingled and Lila flinched at the sound of glass crunching under their feet.

"We'll take your car. Go to the passenger side."

There was no one in sight. A fact that Lila was both thankful and sorry for. The last thing she wanted was for anyone to be hurt, but right now, she was praying for a miracle.

Shane. Shane. Shane.

His name repeated in her head like a mantra, a supplication to the gods, perhaps. She didn't want to die, but this man, he would kill her. Of that, she had no question. He had been willing to beat to death three people, and set a house on fire, when only one woman had been on his list. That was enough of a reality check for her.

She stumbled, her legs going rubbery with fear as the man used the fist coiled in her hair to walk her forcibly to the passenger side of the car, open it, and climb inside as he climbed in behind her, forcing her into the driver's seat.

Her legs were twisting, struggling to get past the steering wheel and into the bucket seat of the tiny commuter car when the sound of tires screeching in the street and her attacker's momentary lapse of focus gave her the one opportunity she had to fight back. She pulled her one free leg back and slammed a foot into the man's chest. It sent him flying back out of the car and into the still-open door. The pistol barked one bullet out, sharp, loud, and Lila felt the heat of it tear through her side, a line of fire. The force of the bullet slammed her forward and her head cracked against the glass of the driver's side window, her body spasming, a fountain of pain washing over her.

A roar, then. Shane. His mouth contorted In rage, fear, as the sound of a gun clattering to the ground and a fist connecting with meat over and over ensued. Lila saw none of this. A rushing in her ears, the unbelievable pain in her side, and her aching skull were taking center stage in her now fading consciousness.

Tick, tock.

Wetness. Her entire middle felt like it was on fire. She touched the wetness, brought her hand up to her face and stared at it, her vision blurring.

Water? No. Blood.

The sound of a fist hitting meat had stopped. Gentle hands touching her. In the distance, sirens.

"Lila, stay with me, baby. Stay with me." Shane sounded so sincere, so... scared. The sirens grew closer. He pulled her out of the car, into his arms.

In her head, a familiar song played. She enjoyed playing it on repeat while writing.

We are here, and then we go.

"Easy come and easy go," Lila muttered.

"Shh, Baby. Hang on, I'm getting you help."

God, she was so *cold*. She could feel Shane's warmth, his hand pressing down on her side caused another dizzying burst of agony.

"I'm in the fire, but I'm still cold."

The sirens blasted through the air. Their lights split the gloom of the encroaching night. So bright. Voices, more voices, movement.

"Stay with me, Lila." Shane said. Did she hear his voice quaver?

"Police! Do not move!" A man shouted.

"I have a gunshot victim here, officer. Caucasian female. Age twenty-six. Pulse is 130. No other medical conditions." Shane's voice again. To anyone else, he would sound calm, but she could sense the urgency in his voice.

"The future's bright, lit up with nowhere to go."

"Lila? Lila!" Shane's voice faded. The lights, so bright, slipped away at the end of a long tunnel.

The world went black.

Time for a Change

- Shane -

Shane slid into the seat of the diner. Here, in the middle of Podunk nowhere, was where Jack has asked to meet. A strange destination, but then, the last few months had been strange overall. It wasn't something he could put into words, but it felt like something had changed for Jack in the last year, and especially in the last few months. His normal base of operations, the sprawling multimillion dollar home in the L.A. hills, where Shane had first come face to face with the man who would later become his boss, was now in various off the beaten path locations all over the country. And far more often, not meeting at all. A phone call from a new number, a quick text. In the six years that Shane had known Jack, the last year had deviated from the norm.

Perhaps that was why Jack had asked to speak with him. His gut twisted at the thought of the discussion ahead of him. Jack would have a new assignment for him, and he was going to have to turn it down.

Ever since the night in the bookstore, and the fear he had seen in Lila's eyes, he knew what the answer had to be. And it wasn't just that he owed Jack Benton for the opportunity, the life he had led for the past six years, it was his very freedom that he owed him as well. Jack had been within his rights to make sure Shane ended up in prison, but he hadn't. He had instead offered him a job, one that had paid him very well, and showed him a life he had only dreamed about.

It wasn't a straightforward thing to walk away from. He had been, until Lila Benoit entered into the picture, rather satisfied with his life. But now?

Now I can't stop thinking about the life I could have with her. One where I wouldn't just fit her in between assignments, but where I would wake up next to her every morning.

"If you were to change careers, what would you do?" Lila had asked him yesterday, her body spooned into his.

"Well, I hoped to be an oncologist. It would be nice to get back into medical school, I guess. I mean, if I even could. I had planned on either working in cancer research or treating patients."

"You could do it; you know. You are meant for more than this bodyguard work, Shane. I'll bet Jack Benton would even help you if you asked. He's got all kinds of connections."

Shane had shook his head. "I can't ask for that." He had felt her sigh. "What?"

"Men can be foolish, prideful creatures."

He had laughed. "I'll show you something I'm quite proud of."

The waitress appeared, coffeepot in hand, replacing the memory of their encore with a crooked, gap-toothed smile. She was older, edging into her fifties, and the deep lines on her face betrayed the evidence of a hard life. "Coffee, sweetheart? Something to eat?" Her eyes widened as Jack slid into the booth opposite Shane and smiled up at her. "Oh, well, hello there. Coffee? Pie? Me?"

"I'll take a coffee and your house special." Jack answered, ignoring the last offer. He smiled again and winked at her.

"Coming right up, darling. And anything for you?" She asked, turning back to Shane.

"Same for me, thanks."

"Okay, well, my name is Jane and you just holler if you need anything." She paused and gave Jack a come-hither look. "Anything at all." Then she sauntered away with an extra swing to her bony hips.

Shane suppressed a snort of laughter. Lila referred to him as the silver fox, and apparently, she wasn't far off.

Jack sipped from the black tar in his cup, winced, and set it down. "I'll stick to water."

Shane sipped from his own cup and had to agree. It rivaled Lila's attempts and producing something worse than nuclear waste. How anyone could screw up coffee so bad, he did not know, but the coffee could etch a hole in the Formica. He pushed it away.

"You asked to see me."

Jack tapped his nails on the table and leaned back. "How is she?"

"Lila? She's... healing."

"Liam kept me updated," Jack said, shaking his head in wonder. "How the bullet missed any major organs, despite the close range and being lodged inside, is a damned medical miracle."

"It was. Well, that and a Taser. The bullet would have caused organ damage if it hadn't been slowed when it hit the Taser. Once they pulled the pieces out and gave her a transfusion, she was in the clear. She's recovering well."

"I saw too that the police chalked it up to a burglary gone wrong, but the perp's prints matched some cold case on the west coast. The courts plan to extradite him to California after his sentencing here. He won't be out on the streets for a very long time." Jack added.

Shane's guts churned. Jack was making nice, asking after her, but now he was going to talk to him about another assignment, and Shane was going to have to tell him no. Despite going around and around it in his head, he still felt unready. Meeting Jack had changed everything. He knew he had savings enough to last the two of them for a year, possibly even three. He could live simple. Shane certainly had before he worked for Jack. Hell, he lived out of a duffel bag most of the time already. It wasn't his way of living that had him in knots, or even making ends meet in the future. It was the thought of leaving a guy who had sought him out, trusted him, and depended on him, in a lurch.

I can't keep doing this, though. Lila needs me, and I need her.

The memory of the panicked flight to the hospital filled his mind. When she had woken up from surgery, he had been there, holding her hand. He'd promised her he would never leave her side again. And he hadn't, not during her stay in the hospital or the weeks after. Not until now.

"It's good that you were there. You saved her life." Jack's eyes bored into Shane's and Shane looked away, clenched onto the coffee cup. The memory of those terrifying moments brought to the forefront of his mind. It had been four weeks now, and he still hated to leave her side, even for an instant. The heat from the hot coffee cup burned his skin and he let go, staring at the reddened flesh, remembering the blood on his hands.

Never again.

"I can't accept another assignment, Jack. I'm... uh, I'm done." The words came out easier than he thought they would.

"I know."

"I mean, not just now. I can't do this job anymore." Shane persisted.

"I know." Jack's tone was calm, matter of fact.

Shane jerked his head up, stared at his boss.

Jack smiled wryly. "Honestly? I'm surprised it has taken you this long to say it."

Shane blinked. "You knew?"

Jack shrugged. "I suspected. And after the bookstore, well, you didn't leave her side. That made it pretty clear what I needed to do."

Shane felt as if the floor was shifting under his feet. "What do you mean, what you needed to do?"

The waitress was back with two plates of greasy eggs, bacon, and a rather gray version of biscuits and gravy. It looked rather off-putting, but it smelled delicious. Jane smiled lasciviously at Jack while barely sparing a glance in Shane's direction.

"Here you go, you two. Can I get you anything else? Anything at all?" she asked, her eyes laser-focused on Jack.

"Thank you, Jane. I think we are good." Jack answered, a broad smile on his face for the aging waitress. Shane half-expected her to leap into Jack's lap. She looked hot to trot.

"Okay, well, you just give me a holler if you need anything." She slid a ticket onto the table and Shane could see she had written her name and what looked like a phone number before she walked away slowly, glancing back with something that looked like hunger and longing. Jack seemed oblivious.

The older man looked over the food and then slid the plate aside. He reached into his briefcase and pulled out a large legal envelope.

"Before I hired you, I had Azule provide a detailed history for you. Just as I would any potential employee." He slid the envelope over to Shane. "You have talents that are not being utilized. I knew when I hired you it wouldn't be forever, and I realize that, considering recent events, your future lies elsewhere."

Jack picked up the cup of coffee and tried sipping it again. While it might have cooled slightly, the taste had not improved if Jack's expression was any sign.

"Ugh, that really should come with a warning label."

"What are you saying, Jack?"

"I'm saying that there is no new assignment, Ellis. Well, there is, but it isn't one as a bodyguard. And honestly, it isn't for *you* so much as it is for *Lila*. I need someone to manage a property for me in Anchorage. I rarely visit. If I do, the guest room downstairs will suffice." Jack sipped his water and pointed at the envelope. "Go ahead, open it."

The envelope was stuffed full of paperwork. Here was a recommendation from a former teacher, no two, one of them a now retired cancer researcher who Shane had studied under. He scanned it, noticed a highlighted sentence, "best student I have ever seen in the medical program."

How had Azule found Dr. Botta? There were copies of his transcripts up to the time he had had to drop out to take care of his mother. An envelope, several other letters, and real estate brochure for a lavish wood home in Anchorage. Shane took a moment to stare at the house. It was beautiful, sprawling over and down the side of a hill. He could see a large pond, and the stunning views of the ocean close by. Edged by the forest, it looked private and spacious.

"I don't understand." Shane said, frowning.

"Keep reading." Jack picked up a fork and cut into the biscuits and gravy, scooping a bite into his mouth. His eyebrows raised in surprise and his fork dug out more.

Shane returned to the papers. A letter caught his attention. They addressed it to him, and the letterhead read University of Alaska Anchorage. His eyes shot up to Jack's.

"This is an acceptance letter. To their medical program. But how..."

Jack chewed, swallowed, and pointed back at the papers. "Keep reading."

Shane's eyes returned to the papers in front of him. It was a full-ride scholarship, all expenses paid. He moved to another letter, one addressed to Lila. This letter was offering her full use of the Anchorage house in the pictures, all utilities paid in exchange for her management of the residence, as well as a small monthly stipend.

"Any repairs will be covered as well." Jack added in between mouthfuls of food. "You should try the biscuits and gravy. They are really quite good."

"Jack, I... I don't know what to say."

"There's more. Keep going."

A separate envelope with his name on it, sealed, read "severance bonus" in Azule's meticulous script. Shane opened it and gaped at the amount. It was twice the amount he had set aside in savings, a stunning six-figure check.

Shane's mouth dropped open in shock. His eyes shot up to Jack.

"Really, try a bite of the biscuits and gravy." Jack scraped the last bite into his mouth and sighed with contentment. Then he reached into his pocket and pulled out his wallet, laying a crisp hundred-dollar bill on the table next to the tab. He extended his hand to Shane.

Shane took it, his mind struggling to keep up.

"Ellis, have Ms. Benoit call me and let me know if she doesn't want the job. Otherwise, I'll expect her to start next week. There's really not much to it, and hopefully will give her the time she needs to work on her novels. I do hope you will keep in touch. I look forward to hearing how you are doing in your studies and with Ms. Benoit."

Jack's grip was firm.

"It, this, I..." Shane struggled to put his whirling emotions into words. It felt as if his boss, well, now former boss, had stepped inside of his mind and read his thoughts. He had certainly done his research. Shane was being handed everything he could have ever possibly wanted or dreamed of.

Jack's voice softened. "Shane, it's time for you to claim your future. Make a difference in the world. Do it for your mother, and yourself, and all the rest of those who will benefit from your future work in cancer research. If you do this, that is all the payment I will ever need."

He slid out of the booth, stood, and clapped Shane on the shoulder. "Take care of yourself, Ellis." Then he turned and waved at the waitress and out the door, the bell ringing shrilly as he did.

Shane sat there in shock, staring at the papers before finally gathering them up carefully and placing them back in the envelope. He hadn't expected the meeting to go like it had, not at all.

Anchorage? College? Full ride? Holy shit.

He picked up his fork and tried the biscuits and gravy. Despite its grayish hue, Jack was right. It was damned good. Jane returned to fill his water, her lined face filled with disappointment. That changed the instant Shane pushed the hundred-dollar bill toward her and told her to keep the change.

The phone in his pocket buzzed, and he pulled it out and answered it.

He could hear the worry in Lila's voice. "Hey, how did it go? Where are you?"

"At a diner. Would you like me to bring you something?"

"Nah, just wondered how it went."

She hadn't pressured him or given him an ultimatum. But after everything that had happened, she didn't need to. He knew things had to be different. He could tell from her voice that she was waiting for him to tell her he was leaving again.

"Actually, it went really well. I have something to show you. I think it's going to blow your mind."

Anchorage

- Lila -

The Crow's Nest at the Hotel Captain Cook was pricey, but it was a celebration, after all. Lila's new book, *Burning Desire*, had blasted up the Amazon charts and was busy knocking off the competition and hitting new heights with each day. It had been hard to peel her eyes away from the sales charts as they ticked away, showing sale after sale after sale. There was work to do and the third book in the series wouldn't write itself.

Still, when Shane had insisted on taking her somewhere special to celebrate, she had been eager to go, even if it meant stepping out into the sub-zero temperatures.

The surprise had included a hotel suite with views of the city, and a gorgeous black dress and high heels. Sitting across from sexy pecan pie Shane Ellis, Lila felt as if she were walking on clouds. It had been over six months in this city and she still couldn't believe her luck. Their lives had changed completely. Now Lila's days were filled with writing and long walks in the woods. Shane remained buried in textbooks and back-to-back classes.

That Jack released Shane from his contract with a six-figure bonus made Lila's eyes bug out. But then he went even further, and secured Shane's entrance into the University of Alaska Anchorage, with a full-ride scholarship in their doctoral program.

The six-figure bonus, along with free housing, utilities, and her small stipend, would allow them to make ends meet while Shane finished his studies.

Certainly, Anchorage Alaska had never been high on Lila's list of destinations. Except for three short months each year, she was perpetually cold. This far north, the summers were short and intense. Now that it was winter, the hours of sunlight were a short-lived affair, dwindling to under six hours on the solstice, before slowly increasing again. By the mid-summer solstice, that would turn into 22 hours of sunlight. Right now, in early January, summer felt impossibly far away.

The city was beautiful, however, and so was the surrounding landscape. The house that Jack had asked her to be a caretaker of was a new build. It nestled on the edge of acres of private forest trails with a stunning view of the ocean. Here she felt safe. No hitman, no one who knew who Marie Trebuchet, romance author extraordinaire, truly was. And she liked that. It had certainly fed her popularity. Mystery author, no photographs, no book signings, just romantic thrillers that had women and men obsessively turning pages late into the night.

Lila had officially requested to be removed from Witness Protection after learning there would be no trial. A mysterious fire in the records room, and the deaths or disappearances of several key players there at Kurgen, had ensured that there would never be the closure she hoped for. And the shadowy organization hiding behind it? The one pulling the strings on the hitmen, the one that Jack had referred to as the Indalo? Quiet.

Jack had warned them that the shadowy figures who pulled the strings were at work on other things. Like a hydra, cut off one head, and the Indalo would grow two more.

Lila couldn't help but wonder if Jack had an ulterior motive in his desire to help Shane with his medical degree. Was he hoping Shane could shed more light on these supposed drugs that Happy Haven was giving to some of the unwitting residents? Watchdog agencies had been warned, but nothing had shown up, no sign that what Denise had overheard was actually true.

You don't kill someone if they are lying, however. You kill them to stop the truth from coming out.

"What are you thinking about?" Shane asked, his hand on hers. It was warm, and it enveloped her smaller, slender one. He stroked it gently, slowly, sensuous. Her body responded, heat flushing her cheeks and traveling down, down.

"I was a million miles away." She pulled her hand away. Reached for her glass and sipped the wine. It was sweet and bubbly, perfect. If he kept touching her hand like that, she might need to take him with her to the ladies, lock them in the stall, and demand he do dirty things to her.

"Thinking of your millions of readers already screaming for the next book?"

Lila shook her head. "I was thinking of, you know, Voldemort." Their own private codename for the Indalo. They had been using it for months, ever since helping Denise. As Jack had astutely pointed out, you never knew for sure when someone could be listening.

Shane groaned. "Lila."

"No, no, really. It's okay. I was also thinking that Anchorage isn't quite the frozen hellscape I imagined it would be." She pointed out the window, where thick snow was now falling, "Well, okay, maybe it's a frozen hellscape *now*, but it has its times of majestic beauty. It really does. And I'm with you, so..."

She lifted her glass again, sipped, and leaned forward conspiratorially. "Tell me, Mister Sexy Pecan Pie, are you having the pork chop with cipollini onion and hazelnuts, or the prime fillet with swiss chard and fondant potato?"

He matched her, raising an eyebrow and giving her a look that turned her insides to jello. "Neither. I think the Elk Osso Bucco with vegetable pave has my name on it." He leaned back, his eyes sliding down from her face to settle on the firm breasts that peeked out of her low-cut black dress. "And you, I don't see you going for the vegan grain bowl."

"God, no!"

He laughed. It was a long-running joke between them, after all. Lila had the appetite of a linebacker and the frame of a dancer.

"King crab legs?"

"Mm, tempting, but no. I think I'll have the ribeye with crushed fingerlings and broccolini."

"Of course you will."

The server returned with a plate of fresh oysters and plates, topped up their glasses, took their dinner order and departed. Lila slipped off her shoes and ran one bare foot up Shane's leg under the table.

"Oysters, huh?"

His face curved into a playful grin. "To cure frigidity."

"As if!" Lila's laugh drew attention for a moment before the other diners went back to their meals. She took that opportunity to move her toes up, up, up. His eyebrow arched, a slow grin spreading over his face.

Her phone pinged at that moment. She reached for it, even as Shane murmured some objection. "It could be Denise. The baby is due any day now."

She squealed with glee at the photos of a tiny baby swathed in blue. "Oh Shane, it *is* the baby! He was born two hours ago. Just look at him! He's perfect!"

Shane leaned forward to peer at the photo. "Cute little guy." He leaned back in his chair and gave her a contemplative look. The tiny furrow dimpled his brow.

"What?"

"Hm?"

She half-glared at him, tucking the phone back in her purse. "You have a look on your face."

A ghost of a smile as he asked, "What look?"

"I don't have baby fever. It's a myth, you know."

"Is it?"

"Yes. Just because I enjoy seeing a picture of Denise's baby does not mean my biological clock is ticking. I have a book to write."

A slow, sexy smile spread over his face. "Have an oyster." He reached for one himself, added a dash of hot sauce and swallowed it. He held out the plate, winking at her. "I've heard that women can be writers *and* mothers. And, believe it or not, I have burped babies and changed diapers before. I can cook and wash dishes. In a pinch, I can even fold laundry properly." If he were trying to convince her he would be the perfect father to her children, she was already there.

Lila gaped at him. "You just started medical school!"

"Yep, sure did." He reached for another oyster. "Damn, these are good."

"What are you saying, Shane Ellis?"

His face assumed an innocent expression. "What? About the oysters? Seriously, eat some before I devour them all."

"About..." Lila leaned close and Shane matched her, his lips brushing hers as their mouths met. "About having a baby." She whispered after he kissed her half-breathless.

"Eat the oyster."

She did. She stared into his beautiful brown eyes and felt the oyster slid down her throat. As it did, his hand slid up her leg, sending a wave of desire crashing through her.

"Now one more."

It felt like a challenge. Lila wondered if they truly had aphrodisiac properties as the second one slid down after the first. Or was it simply Shane and his sex appeal?

He undressed her with his eyes. "We have ten minutes until the main course comes out." He said, setting his napkin down, standing up, and reaching for her hand.

Lila felt a rush of giddiness overtake her. She took his hand and led Shane to the elegant restroom fifty feet away.

No one seemed to notice. The single occupant bathroom was spacious, a separate stall walled off from a sitting room, where a small couch sat positioned against one wall.

Shane locked the door, his hands roaming across her, his mouth sliding up her neck to the sensitive spot by her ear. Lila moaned in pleasure, her hands caressing him, feeling how hard he was for her. She pulled at his belt buckle, tugging it free and then gasping as his hand reached down to cup her ass and lift her effortlessly in the air, and against the wall, his body crushing her. There was pleasure and pain in it, and Lila moaned as he plundered her mouth with his, stealing her breath away.

The couch might have been nice, but they were not going there. She wrapped her fingers in his hair and pulled him closer, their tongues thrusting. She could taste sea salt and the tang of the hot sauce as he adjusted himself, pulled away any petty encumbrances, and thrust into her. Hot. Hard. Lila's gasp of pleasure muted by his tongue, twisting with hers. One shoe clattered to the floor, the other hung on out of pure spite as she wrapped her legs around him and felt him slide in and out of her. His hands dug into her ass, to the point of bruising, but she didn't care. All that mattered was the feel of them moving as one. His dick was deep inside her, thrusting in and out, their mouths fused. Tongues fucking as hard as their bodies were.

She could feel it coming. The orgasm rushing towards them like a freight train. Inevitable. Unstoppable. They came together. A collision of energy and matter that left them panting. Shane sagged, walked backwards with Lila still in his arms, and collapsed down onto the couch, still inside of her. His breaths came in short bursts, and Lila crumpled against him, the rush of endorphins overwhelming. If she stood up now, her legs would simply not work.

She thought of how they still needed to go back out into the restaurant and slid off of Shane.

"Oh my God." She groaned. "That was. Mm. Yeah." She nestled into the crook of his arm.

"Lila. I want you."

"Shane, you just had me. Give me a minute to recover."

He chuckled softly. "I want you in my bed. In my life. I want you standing there when I get my medical degree. When we buy our first house. I want you to have my children."

"You want to have children with me?"

"Yeah. I'm thinking five, maybe six."

"Oh, hell no," Lila said, scrambling up to stare at his face. "*You* go bear five or six kids. I'll sit here and eat popcorn and watch it go down. It'll be a medical miracle."

He laughed. "Fine. Four?"

"Three, tops. And that's my final answer."

"I can live with that. But we'll have to get married. My mom would have wanted me to make an honest woman out of you."

It was Lila's turn to snort. "I'm plenty honest. Thank you very much. But if you were to propose to me in a future moment and time when we haven't just had sex in a public restroom..."

"You might say yes?"

"I just might."

They lay there for a moment more. And then Lila's stomach rumbled. Shane laughed. "Come on. Your ribeye is waiting for you."

"Mm, sounds wonderful. I'm starving!" She sat up, arranging her dress back down around her. She turned to find him staring at her. "I look forward to taking that dress off completely later."

She gave him a coquettish smile, and they stepped out of the bathroom and returned to their table.

He wanted her. In his life, in his bed, bearing his child. Lila felt a rush of hope. She thought of Denise and her child, and of the news she had received just last week that Kaylee was expecting a child. The past two and a half years had been a whirlwind of change. Some moments had been terrifying, life-threatening. But with Shane by her side, everything felt possible.

The main course was absolutely delicious. Each bite felt like a symphony being played in her mouth. The ribeye was medium-rare, just the way she liked it, and they seasoned it to perfection. The fingerling potatoes were buttery and the broccolini a taste of fresh that lightened the heaviness of the meal.

Lila ate the steak slowly, savoring every bite.

Between Shane's cooking and meals like this, I have zero clue how I don't weigh two hundred pounds by now.

She closed her eyes and sat back, a dreamy smile on her face.

"How was everything?" The server asked, a wide smile on his face. It had been there ever since they returned from their escapade in the bathroom.

"Perfect." Shane answered, dabbing his mouth with a cloth napkin. "I think we are ready for the dessert you recommended."

Lila blinked. Had she heard the server mention dessert? If so, she certainly didn't remember.

"Of course, sir." He slipped away from the table before Lila could protest she was full and couldn't possibly fit a dessert in there as well. She wanted to *fit* into her little black dress, after all.

"Dessert? Really?"

Shane just smiled. "I've heard it isn't to be missed. Just one bite. I'll eat the rest if you don't want it." He reached over and took her hand, squeezing it gently before he released it, and stood as the server arrived, dessert balanced on a tray.

The server set down the dessert in front of Lila. It was a delicate crystal parfait glass filled with chocolate mousse with shaved chocolate and a large strawberry on top. Lila stared at it, confused by a tiny flash of light. The top of the strawberry had been removed and a small hole cut down into it. A multi-faceted sparkle at the center caught the candlelight. Lila's mouth fell open in shock. It was a ring. And not just any ring. A diamond engagement ring.

Shane wasn't standing any more. Instead, he knelt on one knee, his brown eyes nearly level with hers. He took her hand in his.

"Lila, these past few months have been the best I could have ever hoped for. I want to spend the rest of my life waking up next to you. Will you marry me?"

Lila's mouth worked, but no sound came out. Since she had woken up in the hospital, Shane had been by her side every single day. She realized now that he had planned this whole evening well in advance. All the months of back and forth, of heartache and hope, of danger and intrigue, it had all led to this moment, this man in her life.

I should say something.

The words had deserted her, though. Finally, she just nodded, happy tears spilling from her eyes.

Shane's lips stretched into a grin and he reached for the ring, gently lifting it from the strawberry and slipping it onto her left ring finger. It was stunning. The diamond was large, square, and set in an antique band, with white and gold filigreed leaves woven in and around it.

Shane pulled her into his arms, and his lips met hers in a passionate kiss. She tucked her face in the crook of his neck, self-conscious of her tears, as the wait staff and several diners applauded.

"I love you, Lila Benoit." Shane whispered.

"I love you too, Shane Ellis." Lila whispered in return.

"Was it too soon after sex in a bathroom?" He asked, still whispering.

Lila just hugged him and laughed.

Target Acquired

- Indalo -

Lucifer recognized the number on her phone and briefly considered not answering it. To say the person on the other end scared her wasn't entirely accurate. After all, she dealt with seriously dangerous people every day, day in, day out. It was the nature of the business, the terms she had accepted when she allowed them to ink her skin. It wasn't just a job, it was life, with the Indalo. Their gaze, their intent, wasn't directly on her, though. It was on people who were in the way of what they wanted. Lucifer did her job, looked up the information they asked for, gave it to them, and washed her hands of the consequences. Well, mostly she tried not to think of it.

How morally gray is that? Lucifer thought as she stared at the incoming call.

Zella Dean, however, was something far more than dangerous. Lucifer had met her once. A few seconds, a minute tops. That was all the in-person interaction she needed. A few months ago, a quick rap at the door, and Annabelle, her massive Great Dane, had woofed once. The dog fell silent, the hackles of her spine raised at the sight of the petite, dark-haired woman at the door. She hadn't growled at the woman, but she hadn't moved either. Not an inch from Lucifer's side, her blue-gray eyes focused on the visitor, her hackles raised in a hard ridge along her spine. The dog was spooked, and that never happened. If Annabelle sensed something off, then there was something terribly wrong with this petite beauty at her door. Lucifer had thrust the zip drive into Zella Dean's hands, doing her best not to show the fear coursing through her. One glance at the woman's dark, death stare was enough to give her nightmares.

"This is everything I could find." Lucifer found her gaze straying away, then back to Zella. She was beautiful. Long, black hair that fell like a curtain along her back, her eyes a dark brown, with unblemished skin, red lips. No makeup, just natural beauty. Lucifer had found herself attracted for a brief second, despite preferring men. Zella had perfect breasts, an hourglass shape, and a kill count that exceeded most of the others. Beautiful, lethal, and from the reaction that Annabelle was giving off, probably the most dangerous human being Lucifer had ever encountered.

Another dart of the eyes back to Zella and Lucifer watched the woman bar her teeth in what might have been a smile, if it didn't feel more like a threat to her life. Any attraction fell away, changing into fear.

Annabelle whined. The sound of it had made Zella's smile grow wider, and Lucifer had felt the crazy radiating off of her. It had pulsed in the air. In the silence between them. In the distance, Lucifer heard the distant clickety-clack of a passing train, an ambulance siren a few blocks away, and the music from the bar at the far end of the street, the bass thumping. But there, in the space between them, an eerie silence. What the hell did this woman want from her, anyway? Lucifer had given her the information she had scraped together.

"Okay, well, I gotta get back to work."

"What's her name?" Zella had asked, her eyes fixed on Lucifer.

"Who?"

"The dog. What is your dog's name?"

Lucifer had fought the urge to slam the door in the woman's face. She couldn't describe it, other than a sense of dread, fear, and chaos in Zella's presence.

"It's um, Dante." Her stomach twisted, but the lie came smoothly out of her mouth. Lucifer didn't even know *why* she was lying. But the thought of Zella saying her dog's name made her want to hurl, or scream, or run gibbering in fear. Maybe all of it. And all at once.

Zella's mouth still held a smile, but there was nothing friendly at all about it. "Thank you, Lucifer. For this." She waggled the hand holding the zip drive in it. She looked down at Annabelle. "Dante. Huh." She shrugged and walked away and faded into the night.

Lucifer had stood there, peering into the darkness of the alleyway beyond for a minute more, Annabelle pressed against her leg, before finally closing the door. After that, she was too disturbed to do anything except lie in bed with her giant dog. Annabelle had twitched and jerked all night, her doggy dreams on overdrive.

That had been a year or more ago. Since then, Zella had called a handful of times. Always with the same questions, the same eerie, unsettling focus.

Tonight was no different. Lucifer paused the game, picked up her phone, and pressed the green button.

"Lucifer speaking."

"Lucifer. How is... Dante?" Zella paused as she said the name. She always did. And Lucifer couldn't help wondering if Zella knew she had lied.

Of all the stupid things to lie about. Maybe Nyra told her about Annabelle. She was the one who suggested the name, after all.

"Um, fine." Lucifer thought about the person she had been six years ago. Naïve. Stupid. Young. Nyra had been nice to her. Just a voice on the other end of a phone. And while she had known she was working for the black hats, she hadn't really known just how dark it got.

Damned if I didn't learn, though.

"I need you to run an address for me." Zella said after a second's pause.

The rabbit hole was deep. Full of bodies. They never talked about it, these voices on the phone. It was all information requests. And Lucifer had been curious. Too curious. She hadn't used the computer, provided to her by her employers. She hadn't even used the same ISP login. One day, shortly after a disconcerting phone call from Zella, a girl she had only heard of through Nyra, Lucifer had bought a phone, set up the protocols that all good hackers used to make her other inquiries as untraceable as those for the Indalo, and she had tracked what happened after she handed over an address to an Indalo operative. Hacking was nothing. It was the tip of the iceberg.

"Sure, go ahead." Lucifer replied, her voice steady, indifferent.

She typed the address that Zella rattled off. Dug into property records, tracked down the owners of record, dug in. It took seconds.

"It's a subsidiary. One that ties back to Benton."

"Excellent, thank you, Lucifer." Zella purred at the other end. Lucifer could hear the sounds of traffic in the background. A couple laughing. She suppressed a shiver. Lucifer wanted to yell at whoever was walking by, tell them to run like hell. She'd heard about a hit last year, shortly after Zella had visited her and retrieved the zip drive with a list of properties owned by Jack Benton. A family of five had died just for being in the wrong place at the wrong time. Zella had been in the middle of it, of course. Just being *near* Zella was trouble. There was a click and the phone call ended. At least Zella spared any getting to know you chitchat past asking after Annabelle. It would have been even more frightening for Lucifer if she had.

Hard to believe Zella is Nyra's baby sister. She's not like Nyra, not at all. Nyra had been an assassin, just like Zella. She had *trained* Zella. *Maybe I'm just a complete fool, buddying up with a killer and thinking we were friends.* She had been so new, so wet behind the ears back then.

Lucifer almost pitied Adrienne Cenac, or Kaylee Stromm, as she called herself these days. That she had survived a year of being hunted by Zella Dean was mind-boggling. Lucifer figured it had everything to do with Jack Benton's protective detail. Still, it wouldn't be long now. Kaylee Stromm and her rich billionaire boyfriend were running out of places to hide. One of these days, they would slip up, think they were safe, if only for a moment, and that is exactly when Zella Dean would strike. Lucifer stared at the black phone screen to the left of her keyboard.

Annabelle nudged her right hand, a moist nose pushing its way between the mouse and Lucifer's palm. Lucifer gently stroked the top of her dog's velvet soft head, distracted by the reality of her life.

I'm not just a hacker, I'm one of them. I'm a black hat.

And suddenly, days filled with video games and hacking challenges didn't feel as appealing as it once had.

In for a penny, in for a pound, as Gram would say. There isn't any way out. Not really. Lucifer was Indalo now. Whether she liked it or not.

Acknowledgments

To Dori, Kate, and Rachel - my teachers at Independent Learning School who allowed me to avoid all of those pesky grammar lessons out of books and do what I loved so much... *write*. Thank you for allowing me to fly.

To my family - my husband Dave, my amazing son, Alexander, my sweet little girl, Angela, and my adorable bookend baby, Ethan. Each day, every day, you all make me nuts, make me laugh, fill my life with a wealth of emotion and experience, and I can't imagine life without you.

A special thank you to Pearl Jam and their song Pendulum played on repeat during the last part of *Where is She?* Damn fine music and the perfect vibe for writing.

To everyone else. You know who you are (or you should).

Author's Note

Thank you for reading Broken Code! I hope you will take a quick moment and leave a review on your favorite book-selling platform. Reviews help readers take a chance on a new (to them) author.

<u>Places</u> - I like to add in details of places that do actually exist. The Airbnb that Lila had rented for her and Shane actually exists. I looked up local Airbnbs near Sugarloaf Mountain and found this caboose: https://www.airbnb.com/rooms/10125337.

Now, while I have never been to this particular Airbnb, I love cool places like this to choose for my literary destinations. How cool would it be to stay in a caboose?! And if you go, tell them I sent you. Who knows, maybe they will give me a discount on a future stay!

The safe house in Kansas City, Kansas (featured in both Hired Gun and Broken Code) exists. Friends of ours bought it in 2015. And while it would not be appropriate to give the exact location, I can tell you it is enormous and really was built in 1970 by a local judge. I loved visualizing it just as our friends decorated it. The 70s decor intermingles with Gothic and Victorian flair and is absolutely stuffed with furniture.

<u>Connect with me</u> - I write because the stories are inside, begging to come out. At times, it feels as if I have no choice. And I love what I do. I hope you will keep reading, and follow me on Facebook or my author website. Drop me an email at shuckchristine@gmail.com and ask me questions or let me know if you liked a book! If you go to my author

website, you will get to read the first chapter on any of my published books and other experimental *works*.

Here are a couple of links to all of those sites:

Author website: https://www.christineshuck.com/

Facebook Author Page: https://www.facebook.com/Christine.D.Shuck

General Malcontent's Grumbles and Scribbles Facebook Group: https://www.facebook.com/groups/555880424837978.

<u>What's coming next</u> - I am a cross-genre author. I couldn't stay in one lane to save my life, really I can't. I write the way I read - so I've got thrillers, sci-fi, romance, time-tripping, dystopian, and non-fiction. That said, at this very moment, I have the following projects in motion:

1. *The Retirement Home* - a jaw-dropping medical thriller guaranteed to keep you up at night
2. *G581: Zarmina's World* - the last installment of the sci-fi series that began with *G581: The Departure*
3. *Quit Your Job, Change Your Life* - an excellent resource for those considering changing careers, embracing entrepreneurship, or just examining where your life is and how you hope to improve it. I hope to roll out a companion workbook and goals/habits journal at the same time.
4. *The Family* - a nail-biting exploration of adoption, the ties that bind, and how one DNA test tips an adoptive mother's world on its head
5. *Tempting Fate* - a return to Benton Security Services and Kaylee and Jack from *Smoke and Steel*, as they navigate rekindling their romance, unaware that a killer is stalking them. There are at least thirteen books planned for the Benton Security Services series. Patience, Grasshopper, they are coming!

I'm still working out time frames for these, but I'm hoping to see most, if not all, in print and available in the next two years. You can stay up to date by joining my subscriber list here: http://eepurl.com/bwbQAH

Don't miss out!

Visit the website below and you can sign up to receive emails whenever Christine D. Shuck publishes a new book. There's no charge and no obligation.

https://books2read.com/r/B-A-BOLF-ZPXFC

BOOKS 2 READ

Connecting independent readers to independent writers.

Also by Christine D. Shuck

Benton Security Services
Hired Gun
Smoke and Steel
Broken Code
Benton Security Services Omnibus #1 - Books 1-3

Chronicles of Liv Rowan
Fate's Highway

Gliese 581g
G581: The Departure
G581: Mars
G581: Earth
G581 Plague Tales
G581: Zarmina's World

War's End
War's End: The Storm

War's End: A Brave New World
Tales of the Collapse
War's End Omnibus - Books 1-3

Standalone
The War on Drugs: An Old Wives Tale
Get Organized, Stay Organized
Winter's Child
Short-Term Rental Success

Watch for more at christineshuck.com.

About the Author

Fueled by homemade coffee ice cream, a lifelong love of words, and armed with strong female (and male) characters I cross genres like the Ghostbusters crossed the streams in pursuit of the question.

"What is the question?" you ask.

The question is simple. It asks, "What would you do, if..."

What would you do if you were fifteen years old and the world as you knew it fell apart? Would you run? Would you fight? Would you survive? – Meet Jess and her brother Chris in the *War's End* series.

What would you do if you had a chance to live your life over? Not just once, but twice? – Meet Dean Edmonds in *Fate's Highway*

What would you do if everyone you loved was lost to a terrible virus and you faced the real possibility of the extinction of the human race in the dark void of space? – Meet Daniel Medry in *G581: The Departure*

What would you do if hitmen were after you and you had no idea why? – Meet Lila and Shane in *Hired Gun*

If I don't keep you turning pages late into the night, desperate to know what happens next, then I have failed at my job. I'm a Taurus and born in Missouri. That makes me bull-headed and stubborn to boot. I don't believe in failure or mistakes, only learning opportunities and clever conversation. There's not much I won't do to make you burn the midnight oil reading my words while you suffer sleep-deprivation the following day. It's my secret superpower.

Born in flyover country, I've also lived in Arizona and northern California. I am an eclectic mix of snark and oddball humor. My colorful metaphors would make a fishwife blush. I'm an incompetent gardener, a dreamer and doer, in love with old houses and shooting pool, and chief organizer of all thing's household and financial. Feed me tiramisu and I'm yours forever.

Find me on all major platforms by visiting Linktree: https://linktr.ee/christinedshuck

Read more at christineshuck.com.